JOINING THE DOTS

A SCOTTISH COMING OF AGE STORY

PATRICK GEORGE O'KANE

OP

OP

This book is dedicated to Mary - for believing -
and
Charlie - for inspiration.

CONTENTS

Author's Note   7

1. Join the Dots   9
2. Bedrock and The Village   17
3. The Quest   21
4. Amabam   39
5. The Spalding Dot   47
6. Romeo, Romeo...   59
7. Lunch with Mother   71
8. The Revenge of the Sardine   81
9. Sausages   93
10. Christmas Dance   111
11. Troubles Come in Battalions   123
12. Joseph   135

Acknowledgements   147
About the Author   149
Contacts and Links   151

AUTHOR'S NOTE

Joining the Dots: follow the antics of two fourteen-year-old boys who befriend each other in a Scottish comprehensive school during the mid-1970s.

The two lads are sharply contrasting characters: Charlie, the cocky 'gallus' joker, and Danny, the more sensitive and naïve academic.

Much of the hard-hitting, reductive humour is drawn from their verbal sparring and the manner in which they react to the confusing and challenging world they have to confront – parents, teachers, fellow pupils, girls, peer pressure and body image being some of the many problems they have to tackle.

They make friends through their shared interest in music and sport but it is a relationship which is often strained, the conflict arising mainly from loyalty and betrayal issues. Despite the constant threat of bullying and violence from adults and peers in each narrative, the collection celebrates friendship and resilience.

This is not a work that presents the West of Scotland as a place of hopelessness and depression – it is, rather, an affectionate, nostalgic, entertaining and funny rite of passage novella that is, despite the multiple obstacles the boys face, uplifting and life-affirming.

1

JOIN THE DOTS

'Oh ya belter, Danny. That's pure quality, big man. It's got tae be the biggest pluke I've ever seen. I mean, there's more pluke than face goin' on there. Wait, don't move – I've got tae draw this new one on The Map.'

Monday morning, double period, back of the Maths class. This was the weekly ignominy of Danny O'Connell's face being updated inside the back cover of Charlie Harkness' jotter. After a weekend of eating sweets and chocolate, Danny's coupon was always explosive, a landscape of pustulant volcanic activity, a shining beacon of vermilion that inevitably attracted attention and derision in equal measure.

As Charlie guddled in his pencil case looking for the HB pencil that was his weapon of choice, he merrily interrogated Danny on what had evidently been a Herculean battle the previous night with The Pluke.

'So did this one put up a fight or was it a pure dead scooshy one?'

'Christ, Charlie, do you really want the gory details. Gie's a break.'

'Aw, come on, Danny, this is what makes S3 Maths class just aboot bearable. Spill the beans, big yin.'

'Well, if you really must know – it was a gusher.'

'Oh, ya dancer. Like, how big was the blast? Bigger than Hiroshima?'

'Well, the art tae bursting a pluke is feeling your way intae the moment. You cannae just pinch it and hope for the best – you've got tae feel for its weak point, press and probe 'til you discover the point of least resistance, know what I mean?'

'No, Danny. Huvnae a scoobie. Never had one single spot on my face, ever.'

'Aw, shut it. Anyways, once you think you've got the pressure point, you position yersel' side-on tae the mirror, close your eyes and squeeeze.'

'Why close yer eyes?'

'Well you don't want splashback do you. The pus comes flyin' oot yer boat race at a phenomenal rate and when it hits the mirror it pure splats all over the place. Especially if it's a Mount Vesuvius like this wan was.'

'Sair?'

'Aye, it nips a fair bit when you burst it but better oot than in.'

'Is that no what they say aboot farts?'

'Aye, well, same principle, different result.'

Like a portrait artist, Charlie held up his beige jotter next to Danny's left ear. His eyes darted between boy and book. A very crude outline of a face was sketched onto the inside page but it had very little physical resemblance to O'Connell's actual visage. That was not the point of the exercise.

'Jesus, Danny, you must have been piggin' oot on the chokky bars of late. There's a whole new batch that's hatched.'

The spotted one looked somewhat crestfallen, guilt and self-disgust battling it out for dominance.

'I cannae help it, Charlie. I've got a real taste for the cream eggs – I love sooking the gooey bit and if you eat them with a packet of plain Golden Wonders, washed down wi' some raspberry Creamola foam, geez, ye cannae whack it.'

'You huvnae any self-control, Danny, that's yer problem. Anyway, let's get tae work. I need tae rub out last week's plukes and put in the new ones. Keep yer heid still.'

The 'artiste' took the small rectangular Helix rubber and gently erased the now defunct dots from the previous week. He blew on the page, sending the little specks of dark grey rubbery residue across the varnished wooden desk. Yesterday's blemishes disappeared like snow off a dyke.

'Naw, it's no' just the chocolate. It's also my genes. My maw had bad skin and my sister's got a face like the moon - she even has tae go tae the doctor's and get a special cream.'

'You don't say,' muttered Charlie, his face now deep in concentration as he touched the paper with the tip of the pencil, checking and re-checking that he had placed the dots in the right place.

'Are you near done, Charlie? Gleeson's starting tae look at us a bit.'

'Ach, that old bugger'll be doon the front for a wee while yet. He's always hovering aroon Anne-Marie Reardon like a wasp on a jeely piece.'

'I wouldnae call her a jeely piece, Charlie. I think she's more like a lovely fairy cake wi' a sprinklin' o' iced sugar on top.'

Charlie stopped sketching for a split second and gave Danny a withering stare.

'You really are full o' crap sometimes, Danny. You honestly think you've got a chance wi' somebody that classy lookin' when you've got a mug like this.'

He held up the jotter and showed it to his subject, the new spots having been sketched onto the plain paper with all the care and attention of a master craftsman.

'And now, Danny me boy, the moment of truth. From this

acne-ridden abomination, what shape shall emerge? It's JOIN THE DOT time, my favourite moment of the week.'

Like the captain of a ship on the high seas, Charlie took his ruler and plotted a chart between the numerous spots, turning the jotter this way and that, coaxing order from the apparent chaos of the speckled galaxy on the page.

'Well, look at this. If I join this dot tae this, I get somethin' that looks a bit like The Plough. Don't take this the wrong way, Danny – I'm not a Harry Hoofter – but you've got a heavenly face. I'm sure I could work in The Centaur if I tried hard enough.'

'Harkness, what the hell are you doing, boy?'

Mr Gleeson, a short squat, little bull terrier of a man was standing over the two boys, glowering at them.

'You're supposed to be on page 47 doing algebra. What the heck is this nonsense?'

He picked up Harkness' jotter and held it between thumb and forefinger as if it was a dirty handkerchief.

'Geometry, sir. I was just joinin' up the dots on Danny's face tae see what shape I could get. It's all very mathematical sir.'

Gleeson raised a sceptical eyebrow, placed the jotter on the desk and stared at the configurations on the page.

'You know, Harkness, you're a pain in the backside but you might be onto something here... I can see a parallelogram in all of this – maybe even a hexagon. Right, everyone, put your pencils down for the moment. Harkness is going to take the lesson, now.'

With supplicant eyes, O'Connell pleaded with Gleeson.

'Sir, this is my face we're talkin' aboot. This isnae fair.'

'Shut it, O'Connell. It's not every day you can say that your kisser has been used as a visual aid. If I can find ways to de-mystify the wonders of geometry to a bunch of cretins like you, then I will use whatever it takes.'

Danny was aware that 34 pairs of eyes were scanning his

countenance, processing the spotty tumult of his features. It's a strange quirk of the human condition that in moments of mortification, when the whole world seems to notice you and you alone, the mind has a way of narrowing its focus from the macro to the micro. At the front of the class, he became aware of two dazzlingly blue diamonds glittering in his direction – the delectable Anne-Marie had paused in her pursuit of academic excellence for a brief comedic distraction, her face a curious mixture of pity, amusement and curiosity. Danny briefly caught her eye, then instantly blushed: not a slight reddening of the cheeks but a furnace heat of industrial proportions. It was so hot, he felt his plukes about to explode.

'I'll never forgive you for this,' muttered Danny as Charlie stood up and strode purposefully to the front of the class, jotter held aloft like a trophy.

For the next ten minutes, Danny watched as the bold Harkness explained the methodology behind his maths. The boys guffawed with hyperbolic gusto, the girls glanced at the subject with mock compassion, barely stifling giggles. Having joined the dots on the blackboard, he placed the chalk on the teacher's desk then picked up Gleeson's measuring stick, pointing it at the huge face leering out at the attentive pupils.

'And, as you can see from this week's shapes, we've got an astrological theme – The Plough and, with a bit of imagination, The Centaur. Thank you for listening and I hope Mr Gleeson can make this a Monday morning tradition.'

'Don't push your luck, Harkness. We've wasted enough time. An amusing diversion for today but no more of this nonsense from now on, understand?'

Charlie shrugged his shoulders.

'Your loss, sir.'

The class tittered.

'OK, Harkness, you can sit down now.'

Picking up his jotter from the desk, he started to move to the back of the class.

'Sorry, Harkness. Come back out. There's just one more thing I want you to do.'

Charlie turned and strode to the front, happy to be given the oxygen of attention yet again.

'If you could put the jotter on my desk for a moment... thank you. Now, put out your hand.'

The cocky Harkness' smile immediately evaporated. Silence descended on the class. The imperative 'Put out your hand' was like a sorcerer's spell, turning day into night, joviality into oppression.

'But sir...'

'You heard what I said. And if you hesitate one more time, I will double what you're going to receive.'

Harkness' shoulders stooped for a brief second then he straightened up as he held out his right hand, face impassive. Experienced in the dark arts of corporal punishment, he knew that any sign of emotion could be interpreted as weakness or defiance, both of which could be rewarded with extra force or six of the best. Gleeson smiled and stood straight on to Harkness. He paused for a second, savouring the suspense, drinking in the tension like a fine wine. Slipping his right hand into his tweed jacket, he slid his stubby fingers upwards towards the shoulder. The class all knew this is where he secreted his Lochgelly and, with the speed of a professional gunslinger, he whipped the tawse out of its 'holster', raised it high over his right shoulder and lashed at Harkness' outstretched hand. The force of Gleeson's strike made the boy's arm collapse downwards, his face momentarily wincing. The distinctive slap of leather on tender flesh never failed to draw flinches from an audience, the class shifting uncomfortably in their chairs. Gleeson twitched the belt upwards, a silent indication that

Harkness was to extend his hand again – and, again, that downwards motion, that unique thwack.

'Left hand, now.'

The economy of Gleeson's movement combined with the accuracy of his aim revealed an expert, a master of the medium. Receiving four of the belt from Gleeson would always hurt; receiving six, though, would be a badge of honour. But today Harkness was to be denied that honour – only four.

'Let that be a lesson, young man. First of all, don't waste time at the back of my class. Secondly, if there is any time to be wasted, I'll do it. Thirdly, don't make such a mess of your school jotter. Fourthly, don't be so presumptuous as to think you can tell me what I'm going to teach and when. Four transgressions; four of the belt. Simple equation. Right now, pack up and bugger off.'

The bell rang just as Charlie arrived at his desk, hands thrust under his armpits. Raw, throbbing and slightly shaking, he held them out in front of Danny who stared miserably at them.

'Sorry, Charlie.'

Charlie smiled and gingerly started to place his rubber and pencils in the pencil case. Danny helped him to pack away his jotter into his Adidas bag.

'What have you got tae be sorry aboot? I suppose I asked for that. Tae hell with Gleeson. Let's go get a sausage roll.'

The two boys picked up their bags and headed for the door.

'Hey,' said Charlie cheerfully as they left the room, 'I bet Anne-Marie Reardon was dead impressed with that. I think I'm in there.'

2

BEDROCK AND THE VILLAGE

I f the past is a foreign country, then Clydebank in 1976 could be classified as an alien outpost at the furthest reaches of the universe. If Mr Spock had been orbiting in the good ship Enterprise back then he would have run a scanner over the area and undoubtedly declared, 'It's life, Jim, but not as we know it.' In fact, to be absolutely accurate, the heroes of our story weren't strictly Bankies. They were from two outposts to the outpost.

Charlie Harkness hailed from Duntocher, a few miles up the road from Clydebank. Known locally as The Village, this rather quaint, almost romantic title belied its true nature. There was nothing particularly rural or idyllic about Duntocher. The West End, where the hard-core natives lived, was a grimly grey hotch-potch of carbuncle-ugly tenements and squat terraced houses, all council owned, while the East End was more upmarket, an estate of privately owned houses, which had been given the nickname Spam Valley, the tinned processed meat allegedly being all that the 'toffee-nosed gits' who lived there could afford on account of the mortgages they had saddled themselves with. Getting into debt was still frowned on back then – the Thatcher revolution was still a few years off – so any opportunity to put a verbal pin in the balloon of aspiration or pretension was taken at every opportunity. Inverted snobbery was in rude health in the west of Scotland in the 70s.

To be fair on Duntocher, it did have some proper history it could bleat about and they lorded it over neighbouring schemes. It boasted a section of The Antonine Wall, the Romans having decided that this was as far North as they dared to go, weather and natives being crucial factors in their resolution that they would go no further. If you had fallen foul of a Roman Emperor you were banished to Duntocher with the mission to quell any revolting natives. Scrolling rapidly through the centuries, the village had also worked two mills during the Industrial Revolution but post WW2, council houses sprang up to house workers for John Brown's shipyard and Singer's factory. However, these manufacturing powerhouses were merely places of employment. For your average man, one's true calling was found at the bottom of a glass. The most important buildings, by far, were the two immensely popular pubs – O'Neill's and O'Donnell's – the all-pervasive demon drink simultaneously being the social glue and the anti-social friction of the community. At the end of a week of hard labour or mind-numbing banality, the refuge of masculine camaraderie gave purpose to life. However, many a week's wages would be blown on a Friday night; many a child went hungry if its mother failed to intercept her spouse before the coffers of Mr Tennent or McEwan were swollen to bursting point.

One thing you could say about the place, it had character, a personality, a roiling swagger about it that said, 'We know who we are and where we've come from and we don't really care what you think.'

And then there was Faifley, the place where Danny O'Connell lived.

The town planners of Danny's place of residence had built a by-pass around the housing scheme of Faifley, a charisma by-pass, slam-dunking an almost Soviet style architectural brutalism on the hilly landscape overlooking the Clyde Valley. The West End Duntocherites, never slow to denigrate a nearby location, called it Bedrock. Indeed, Danny, on moving from primary to secondary school had been asked, without a hint of sarcasm, by a fresh-faced Duntocher kid in S1, if they all lived in caves up there in Faifley and whether the wheel had been invented. In all honesty, a cave might have been more of a des res than the tenements that had been erected in the late 40s, early 50s. Post WW2, there was a genuine feeling that the state was going to look after the common man, that providing affordable housing for the working populace would eliminate the fear and anxiety of having to own property and all the financial worries associated with it. In principle, it was a good idea, and many a decent family moved into these dwellings with the best of intentions to make it work. However, the ugliness of the architecture, the decline of traditional industry and the cancerous growth of unemployment ate away at the social cohesion of the place. That, coupled with the fact that there was no centre, no community hub meant, by the mid-70s, it was a holding pen for those that wanted to move on or a dumping ground for problem families from Greater Glasgow. On the positive side, it had two primary schools – one Catholic, the other Proddy – and two churches – one, Catholic, the other Proddy – and a Co-op. It did have one pub, a flea-bitten hovel that only the desperate frequented.

Apart from that, nothing of note, nothing to stimulate the mind or body, nothing to be proud of, nothing to inspire a native to puff out their chest and say, 'I'm from Faifley.' No one even knew what to call someone from Faifley – was it a Faifleyite, a Faifleyer, a Faifle, a Fleyer – but then again no one really boasted that they came from there so it wasn't really an issue. The Duntocherites were happy just to call them cavemen.

So, from these two outposts of the universe came our likely lads – or should that be unlikely lads – Charlie, a product of the gallus mind-set of The Village; Danny, a martyr to acne, a character in search of identity.

3

THE QUEST

As the sun sank beneath the Old Kilpatrick Hills, casting a golden glow over the West End of Duntocher, four furtive figures emerged from a tenement close in Craigiebank Road.

'Right, how much have we got? If we have any luck, we might have enough for three cans each.'

With the authority of a sergeant major on the parade ground, Charlie lined up the intrepid gang by the garages to the rear of the tenement block.

'Come on, empty yer pockets and see who's where and what's what. I've got 50p.'

First to be inspected was wee Tony Toner who, even in S3, was not so much a dedicated follower of fashion, more a blinkered zealot who could not understand why anyone could not feel passionate about a) wearing the right flares, b) having the perfect shade of Simon shirt or c) choosing the correct height of platform on their shoes. The emergence of the perm and its mullet companion was still in its infancy but, somehow, Tony had a nose for these things – and what a nose it was. The whole of Duntocher had a theory that his mother had 'played away' because no one else in the family had a conk like wee Tony. What he lacked in height he made up for in the snozzle department – his resemblance to a proboscis monkey was quite astonishing. The only problem with the 'playing away' theory was that Tony had a twin brother who looked like the rest in the family so the infidelity supposition lacked any credible evidence. Physically, his brother, Martin, could not have been further from Tony in looks and build. He was at least a foot taller and, where his sibling won in the nasal stakes, Martin's lugs were clearly stand out victors. He was like the illegitimate son of an illicit coupling of Prince Charles and a Toby jug. But genetics will always show its hand. The two boys had one thing in common. Their combined IQ score would have had them hovering between the moronic and the imbecilic, both languishing in all the bottom sets at school, both blissfully unaware that the academic world existed, such is the sweet ignorance of the terminally stupid. But they were harmless enough lads who did everything together and whose familial loyalty was second to none.

'I spent most of my dosh on gettin' this perm at the weekend, Charlie. I've only got 10p.'

He reached into his pockets and held out his meagre offering.

'God sake, Tony. We agreed last week that this was gonnae be the night we got marokulous and we'd save oor pocket money.'

'Aye, I know, Charlie, sorry but wee Sarah doon the hairdressers said I'd look great wi' a perm and I couldnae say no. And you have tae admit – it was well worth it. I look like the cat's bollocks.'

'It's dog's bollocks, ya fud – or cat's pyjamas, one of the two. But haud on a minute, naw, naw and triple naw – a perm on a man looks right daft. That's for auld women. It'll never catch on. You'd look better wi' a paper bag o'er yer heid. Mind you, they'd have tae cut a bit oot of the front tae let yer nose oot.'

'No need to be like that, Charlie. I said I was sorry. Maybe Martin's got some spare cash, eh Martin?'

'Aye, well ye see Charlie I had 50p this morning and I was right up for this so I was and my dad came intae oor room before I got up and went intae my trooser pocket and took my money and said he was on a sure thing at the bookies this afternoon and that he'd pay me back with interest though I don't know what's interesting aboot payin' money back tae somebody so I said tae him this evenin' could I have my money back and he belted me roon the lugs and told me tae mind my own business that it was his money tae begin with and that I should be grateful I had such a generous dad and that he's the man o' the hoose and so that's the story of how my 50p got taken away from me and never returned.'

'In the name of the wee man. I'm givin' up the will tae live here. Whit have you got, then? There must be somethin'. Hand it over.'

Martin rummaged around in his trouser pocket and extracted a silver coin. With a rather sheepish look, he placed it in Charlie's demanding outstretched hand.

'5p. A measly 5p. Whit sort of a Friday night swally are you supposed to have wi' 5p? That'll give you about a third o' a can, Martin. That'll no' get ye pished.'

'I didn't know you could buy just a third o' a can. What'll they think o' next?

Charlie rolled his eyes, then turned to Danny who was hovering in the shadows of the nearest garage, staring morosely at the ground, desperately trying to avoid visual contact.

'And what are you looking so miserable aboot? Don't tell me you're skint as well.'

Danny, with an expression akin to someone with severe constipation, muttered, 'Time's are hard in Faifley, y'know. We're not all as flush as you, Charlie.'

'Whit ye mean by that? Do you think that just cos I brought 50p to the table that my dad's won the pools or somethin'? Don't gie me the big sob story aboot your family not having any dough.'

'I had tae raid my piggy bank tae find somethin'. It took me hours tae winkle oot whit was in there. I had tae get one o' my maw's kirby grips and stick in in there and then footer aboot for donkey's ages trying tae squeeze it oot o' the wee slot.'

'And – so – whit's the result? I cannae stand the suspense.'

'2p.'

Charlie stared at him, mouth agape, a walking embodiment of incredulity. He sought confirmation.

'2p?'

With the slightest whiff of insouciance, Danny nodded his head, '2p.'

The moment hung in the air as Charlie desperately tried to compute what the devastating consequences of Danny's lack of liquidity would have on the evening's proceedings. Danny, interpreting the stony silence as an insult to his hard-fought sacrifice, went on the offensive. 'Take it or leave it, mate. That's all my worldly possessions I'm handing over tae you, so you should be thankful for it.'

'You should be thankful I'm not ramming it up your arse, Danny.'

He turned and looked at his wannabe bacchanalians and sighed.

'Ok, let's add this up. 50p frae me – well done Charlie, thank you Charlie, you delivered what you promised Charlie - 10 frae Tony, 5 frae Martin and the truly sterling effort frae Danny – 2p.'

'That's aboot a pound then, innit, Charlie. That's no' bad,' cried Martin excitedly, even though he had given up counting after 60p, the addition of numbers always a challenge of Himalayan proportions.

'Naw, Tony. That's only 67p, a pathetic dribble of o' pish, that's what it is. Never mind. A dribble o' pish is better than nothin', I suppose. At 15p a can, that's one each an' some crisps as well. We'll need some scran tae soak up the booze. My dad says never drink on an empty stomach.'

'Saltn'shake crisps would be good,' declared Danny, 'I love those wee blue bags an' the noise it makes when you shake them an' the way the crisps at the bottom o' the bag taste better than the ones at the top. Like saving the best 'til last.'

'Will you belt up aboot Saltn'shake crisps. You'll be lucky tae get wan swig from my can if you don't shut up, Danny. Anyways, you need tae knock off the crisps on account of yer condition.'

'Whit condition is that?' asked Tony, his powers of observation, razor sharp as always.

'Christ, Tony, look at his coupon.'

Tony examined Danny's face with curiosity. He stepped back in horror, his aesthetic sensibilities rocked to the core.

'Yeuggh. Now you mention it, Charlie, what a mess. You should see a doctor aboot that, Danny. That's pure bowfin'. That would scare the weans on Halloween that would. I'd only go oot after dark wi' a face like that.'

'It is after dark,' mumbled Danny, his eyes downcast, the evening suddenly taking a turn for the worse.

'Right, enough o' this crap. If we don't hurry up, Dodgy Ali's will be shut.'

'That's rubbish, Charlie,' interjected Martin. Dodgy Ali never shuts. And even if he does, you can knock on the back door an' he'll sell you stuff.'

'Aye, fair enough. Anyways, we need tae get a move on. Time tae get blootered – or mildly inebriated as the case may be.'

Charlie led the way, a Pied Piper leading his merry little band to the promised land of something new, something dangerous, something forbidden. For all the bravado and big talk from the boys, this was to be a rite of passage, their first piss-up. They had all tasted alcohol before but it had always been a mere surreptitious slurp from their parents' glasses at Christmas or Hogmanay, nothing like this – a proper, organised 'sesh'.

Suddenly from a narrow space between the last two garages, a tiny figure emerged, a miniscule female humanoid wearing a grubby paisley pattern dress, two grimy knobbly knees poking above scuffed red wellies, an unkempt explosion of dark wavy hair atop a face that had a fleeting and troubled acquaintance with soap. This little urchin would have had a cute button nose if it hadn't been obscured by layers of snot, an adenoidal effluence with an archaeological layering from fresh dark green goo to stale pale green encrustation. Aside from this vision of rhinal loveliness, this diminutive creature had one more outstanding feature. She had the worst squint this side of the Clyde. She was looking at Martin but was speaking to Charlie.

'Hi there, Charlie.'

'Ohh, it's yersel'. Heh Danny, let me introduce you. This is Inch-High-Squinty-Eye. Inch-High-Squinty-Eye, this is Danny.'

'Och, Charlie,' exclaimed the wee poppet while still looking at Martin, 'You know my name's no Inch-High-Squinty-Eye. My name's Maureen.'

'Aye but Inch-High-Squinty-Eye's a far better name. It really suits you.'

'Do you think so, Charlie?'

'For sure. I'd be dead proud tae have a nickname like that. Pure class. Everybody'd know who I was. You're a like celebrity roon these parts, so don't be calling yersel' Maureen.'

'You might be right, Charlie. Anyways, what ye up tae and can I join in?'

'We're off tae get banjoed, if you must know.'

'Can I come?'

'Naw, Inch-High, this is man's work. How old are you anyways?'

'Six and a half, nearly seven.'

'Oh, you'll have tae wait a couple o' years before you can start drinking so away back home and play wi' yer dollies or whatever it is you lassies do wi' yer time.'

'Aww, can I no' just tag along? I willnae be a bother.'

''Fraid not wee one. You toddle off now. Goan enjoy yersel'.'

'Awright, Charlie. See you later. Bye everyone.'

A chorus of 'Bye Inch-High-Squinty-Eye' rang round the walls of the tenement back court.

'And Charlie...'

'Yeh, whit is it?'

'I love you so I do.'

The lilliputian Lulu skipped off into the night shadows as an eruption of laughter and wolf whistles rose into the night sky. All three boys in mock high pitch voices mimicked the love-struck Maureen: 'I love you so I do.'

'Shut it,' snapped Charlie, somewhat discombobulated by Inch-High's declaration of passion. 'Come on; catch a grip. We're supposed to be steamboats by noo.'

Charlie stomped off down the road, the street lights from the tall concrete lampposts reflecting off the tarmac, the tenement blocks either side of the thoroughfare channelling the boys in one predetermined direction – Dodgy Ali's corner shop. No one was quite sure exactly which part of the Indian sub-continent Dodgy was from – in all honesty, no one really cared as long as you could get what you needed at whatever time of the day or night you needed it. The good people of Duntocher collectively wondered if the proprietor ever slept, no one ever having seen him outside of his shop, day or night. The sobriquet 'Dodgy' had been given to him on the basis that the foodstuff he sold was largely detrimental to your health – either canned stuff past its sell-by date or 'fresh' produce somewhat compromised by hygiene violations. It was not uncommon to see Dodgy carving ribbons of cold gammon on his electric meat slicing machine, an Embassy Number 1 fag hanging from his lips, and it was equally not uncommon to see the cigarette ash plop onto the pink oval shapes just before he wrapped them up in greaseproof paper. On returning home, you would always have to brush the grey detritus off the processed meat before slapping it between two slices of Mother's Pride. Connoisseurs of gammon argued that the fag ash added a certain body to its texture. Furthermore, Dodgy was also beloved by the adolescents of the community, largely due to his willingness to sell individual cigarettes to any teenager that wanted to look cool and grown up. Single-handedly he set many a kid on the pathway to a lifetime of nicotine addiction. But business was business.

He was also known to sell alcohol to the underaged, which is obviously why the four brave musketeers were standing on the other side of the road from the shop, pontificating over their next move.

'Who's going tae go in for the booze?' asked Danny, not one of them having planned out the operation to this level of detail.

Four pairs of eyes looked across at the light emanating from the barred windows. A white plastic bag had caught in the roof gutter and rustled in the gentle breeze. Although Dodgy's retail ethics were highly questionable, there was a limit to his opportunism. He had, quite recently, been warned by the police that there was going to be a clamp-down on the sale of alcohol and tobacco to young people. All the shops in the area were on red alert. Being a relatively small place where everyone knew everyone else's business, it was widely known that this was the current state of play.

'Good question, Danny,' said Charlie. 'This is the tricky bit. We've got tae choose someone who looks the part, maybe even someone that isnae well-known aroon these parts.'

'Well,' said Tony, 'Dodgy knows me... and he knows Martin... and he knows you, Charlie. So that just leaves...'

The three Duntocher boys turned and stared at Danny, the outsider.

'Aww, naw, hang on a minute. I didnae sign up for this. I don't want tae get lifted by the polis.'

'It willnae come tae that. The worst that can happen is he just says naw,' re-assured Charlie.

'Aye and then he'll phone the cops and I get put in jail.'

'Don't be daft. And, anyway, Danny, you look the most mature oot of all of us. You're the tallest by far and you have that old man air aboot you.'

'Old man air? What the hell does that mean?'

'Take it as a compliment, especially in this situation.'

'Aye, Charlie's right,' declared Martin. 'We three wouldnae be able tae pull this aff. You're the man, Danny me boy.'

'I agree,' cried Tony, 'Let's have a vote. All those in favour of Danny buying the booze, raise your right hand.'

Three arms shot up in the air simultaneously.

'This is discrimination against Faifley folk, this is. You're pickin' on me cos I'm no' an inbred like the rest o' you.'

'Right Danny. Might I just remind you of your pathetic contribution tae tonight' festivities. 2 pence. 2 measly pence. So I reckon you owe all o'us and owe all o'us big time. So, stop yer whingein', get yer arse across the road and let's get partyin' before we end up old enough tae drink anyway.'

Charlie thrust the money into Danny's hand and pushed him off the pavement in the general direction of the shop. Shoulders stooping, he loped across the road and stopped in front of the door. He looked up at the sign 'Ahmed Ali – Convenience Store'. Butterflies were dancing in his stomach and the sensation was not unlike standing outside a classroom just before an exam. However, there was something a wee bit different about this. He was aware that he was The Chosen One, that the success of the evening was down to him, that he had been given the responsibility to make all of this work. He pushed to the back of his mind a sneaking suspicion that the others were simply playing him, convincing himself that he was the saviour of their collective mission, The Mission to Get Bladdered.

As he opened the door, a little bell rang above his head. There was a movement to his left and a sallow-skinned bearded gentleman wearing a blue apron around his neck stood up behind the counter. There was a fug of smoke around him as he puffed on a half-finished cigarette. He nodded at this figure in front of him, a tall gangly youth with greasy hair, afflicted with some sort of skin condition and wearing polyester charcoal trousers and a bright red cagoul. Danny blurted out a somewhat overly enthusiastic 'Evening,' and Dodgy once again nodded at him, this time narrowing his eyes in suspicion. He was always on the look-out for chancers in his shop, though, to be fair, this particular specimen looked a bit gormless.

'Act cool,' Danny thought to himself, 'You can do this. You're the man.'

He turned to Dodgy Ali and, smiling with as much devil-may-care attitude as he could muster, asked, 'Could you kindly tell me where the Saltnshake crisps are?'

'Third aisle at the back.'

'Thank you so much Mr Ali.'

Danny had decided that calling him Dodgy might ruin his chances of success, even though Mr Ali was quite happy with his nickname, believing that a Pakistani man living in the West of Scotland could be called a hell of a lot worse.

Danny picked up a basket and headed off down the third aisle. Sure enough, he found the Smiths blue and white packets piled in a heap next to the Monster Munch. He picked up two packets and dropped them in his basket. He became aware of two circular mirrors high up in the corners of the store and, being the only customer in the shop, Mr Ali was keeping a wary eye on him. Danny saw that his objects of desire were in the first aisle in the direct sightline of Dodgy and decided that the best form of attack was the indirect approach. He started to wander around the rest of the shop in a nonchalant meander, feigning an interest in the produce, picking up jars of jam and marmalade and examining them as if he was the world's foremost expert on fruit preserves. Having exhausted his powers of observation on Robertson's foodstuffs, he happened to glance out the window. His three amigos on the other side of the road stood with their arms outstretched in exasperation and frustration, their countenances expressing incredulity at the length of time he was taking in purchasing the bevvy. Well, they would just have to wait. He was sticking to his plan. He then found himself in a part of the shop in front of products he had never seen before, alien objects in pink plastic wrappings with the word *Always* imprinted on their shiny surface. He picked up a packet and squeezed it, its texture quite malleable, even spongy, and wondered if whatever was inside it was edible, like giant marshmallows. He lifted it to his nose and sniffed it:

'Are you some sort of weird pervert or are you buying these for your sister? Whatever you're doing please stop pawing at the ladies' sanitary products.'

With Dodgy glowering at him, Danny threw the packet down on the shelf as if he had been stung by a bee.

'Do you have what you came for? If so, please pay; if not, kindly make your purchase and leave. You are starting to irritate me, young man.'

'Sorry Mr Ali. I was just admiring the range of goods you sell. Nearly done.'

Danny decided to bite the bullet and strode purposefully towards the shelves where rows and rows of multicoloured bottles stood in serried ranks – but this was not what he had come for. Right beside the counter, stacked high and proud, was a tower of Tennent's lager cans, Scotland's ubiquitous national drink. This was the golden fleece young O'Connell sought. Without any flicker of hesitation, he extracted four cans from the pile and slammed them on the counter with the air of a man that meant business.

'Four cans of Tennent's, please.'

'Yes, I can see that, young man. And when I say young man, I mean young man. How old are you, sonny?'

Danny was prepared for this one.

'18.'

'What is your date of birth?'

Danny, unfortunately, was not prepared for this twisted line of enquiry.

'Ehhh?'

Now, just as Tony Toner had always struggled with the finer points of addition, Danny O'Connell had never been a genius when it came to subtraction. He screwed up his face and desperately tried to take 18 away from 76. If he had been sharp enough, he would have simply taken 4 away from 62, the year he was born, but this was beyond his mathematical boundaries.

'7th of May, 1957.'

'So that would make you 19 years old, then.'

'No, sorry, 1958.'

'So, you don't know when you were born.'

'No, I mean, yes. I'm not very good wi' numbers. Just ask my Maths teacher.'

Dodgy gave him a withering look.

'Look sonny, you don't look a day older than 14 and I could

have my business shut down because of little eejits like you, so, pay for the crisps and go.'

'Naw, naw, Mr Ali. Ok, I'll be honest and spill the beans. I'm 17 – soon to be 18. I'd look a lot older if it wisnae for my plukes. These spots on my face are concealing a mature adult, a real man – and look at my height. You don't see many 14-year-olds aroon this neck o' the woods nearly 6 foot tall.'

Dodgy mentally acknowledged that as a fact, the vast majority of those in the neighbourhood being of the stunted variety. He examined him again. There was no way he was anywhere near 17, never mind 18. But Dodgy is as Dodgy does. It had been a painfully slow day in the shop and he had not got where he was today – The Corner Shop King of Duntocher – without sealing a deal.

'OK, sonny. I'm a nice man and would not do this for everyone so, just this once I sell you this beer. But you keep your trap shut, you understand. Four cans of Tennent's and two packets of crisps. OK, that's 70p altogether.'

'I've only got 67p.'

'Well, you'll have to put something back.'

'I'll put back one o' the crisps.'

'That's 65p, then.'

Danny handed over the money and then realised that the 2p he had brought to the jamboree was still in his hand. He pocketed it.

'Result!' he thought to himself.

'Thanks, Mr Ali. You have a nice evening.'

'On yer bike, sonny.'

Carrying the cans and the packet of crisps in a dark green plastic bag, he left the shop, head held high, the little bell tinkling behind him.

'What the hell, Danny,' cried Charlie, 'were you asking Dodgy oot on a date or somethin'? That took donkey's years. What a drouth we've aw got noo. Seriously, whit are you aboot?'

'Ye cannae hurry a genius when he's at work, Charlie. I had tae negotiate with Dodgy and these things take time. You wouldnae know aboot that sort o' thing cos you're no mature enough tae pull somethin' like this aff.'

'I've only got one word tae say tae that - bollocks. Right, enough o' the verbal diarrhoea and let's get the night properly started. Follow me, lads.'

Striding out with fresh vim and vigour, the exuberant lads headed further west, like a quartet of hobbits on a quest, an expedition to the furthest reaches of The Village. Their destination was The Secret Place, a site that the teenage Duntocher cognoscenti were convinced adults knew nothing about. Little did the youngsters know, but this hush-hush locale had been used for generations as a rendezvous for all sorts of clandestine activity. Each generation believed they were the ones that had found the spot; each generation grew up and left its hidden delights behind them. Tonight, though, it was our intrepid trailblazers who navigated their way to an expansive bridge that spanned a deep gorge, the bridge itself being part of the A82 dual carriageway, the Great Western Road, whose source was the centre of Glasgow, whose terminus was somewhere north in a remoteness named Inverness, a town that could have been in Outer Mongolia for all the boys cared. However, underneath the bridge was their own terminus, far from the prying eyes of censorious adults and the perfect private place to get plastered. The four of them gathered in a spot that was at once shadowy yet had just enough neon light from streetlights in the distance to allow them to see what was what. They huddled around Danny as he opened the bag and extracted the four cans.

'Did you remember the crisps?' asked Martin, 'I'm Hank Marvin.'

'One packet of Saltnshake comin' right up.'

Danny drew out the crisp poke with a flourish. 'Darraaa.' He held it above his head triumphantly.

'One packet. Is that aw?'

'Well, sorry I couldn't lay on a buffet for yer 67p, Charlie. Jesus, I'm pure overwhelmed by the gratitude boys. Anyway, we can divvy up the crisps later.'

'Aye, fair enough,' replied Charlie magnanimously, 'Let's get tae the important bit.'

He handed a can to each of the boys. All four peered at their individual Holy Grails.

'Which burd have yous aw got?' queried Martin. 'I've got Michelle.'

They gawped at the sirens on the side of the lager cans, comely maidens looking out suggestively at the leering lads, the Tennent's marketing strategy of sticking sexy models on the side of Scotland's favourite beer at once a stroke of genius and a stamp of chauvinism. Not that such niceties worried these boys. The allure of alcohol and the mystique of the female form were seas that they were about to set sail on, with the tantalising promise of landing on the shores of a New World: the glamorous world of The Adult.

'I've got Penny.'

'Mine's is Heather.'

'I've got somethin' called Slyvia. Who the hell is called Slyvia? Whit sort of a name is that?' Tony stared at his can, somewhat irked by the crappy name of his 'burd'.

'Here, let me see,' said Charlie, taking the can from him. 'It's Sylvia, ya muppet.' Charlie stared at her for a few moments. 'She's aw right, actually. Here swap you. You can have Heather.'

'Aye, ok. I couldnae be doin' wi a burd whose name I cannae read.'

'Well nobody's gettin' a haud o' my burd,' announced Danny. 'Penny. She's a doll. And look at the thrupenny bits on her. They're huge.'

They all gathered round Danny and looked at the delights of Penny.

'Whit I wouldnae do tae her,' blurted out Martin.

None of the boys really understood this utterance but they all nodded in agreement, no one having the courage to challenge Martin on what exactly it was he wouldn't do to Penny.

'Ok, lads,' Charlie broke the spell of pent-up sexual tension and confusion and held up his can in front of him, his forefinger clawing the ring-pull, like a soldier about to pull the pin on a grenade. 'Time tae get wrecked. Let's say we open the cans aw at the same time. On the count of three. OK?'

All three nodded in agreement.

'Are we ready? One... two... three...'

'Oi!'

The quartet jumped high in the air.

'Oi, are you Chick?'

Charlie swung round and stared in the direction of the voice.

'Who's that?'

'I said, *Are you Chick?*'

'Aye, who wants tae know?'

'You're Chick the Prick.'

The disembodied voice suddenly took human form, an incarnation simultaneously disorientating and terrifying. About forty yards away, out of the shadows, hurtled a frightening apparition, a wild-eyed demon that had a single distinguishing characteristic – it had only one arm and this arm was rotating like a windmill in a hurricane. What was even more disturbing was that there was a brick attached to the arm and that brick suddenly fizzed through the air, just missing Charlie's skull.

Dropping his can of Tennent's in an instant, Charlie screamed, Run!' All four boys did likewise, turned and sprinted for dear life, leaving Penny, Sylvia, Heather and Michelle face down in the dirt.

'That's it. Run away ya bunch o' poofs. Chick the Prick and he's wee gang o' bum chums. Don't even think aboot comin' back for the bevvy. It's aw mine noo.' A mad cackle rose in the air as the boys disappeared into the back courts of the nearest tenements.

'Who the hell was that?' puffed Danny as they slowed down to a jog, an acceptable distance having been established between the one-armed bandit and themselves.

'That's Puggy Shuggy. A complete bampot. He's in my big brother's year at school – everyone knows he's a psycho. He's probably been followin' us aw evenin'. You dinnae mess wi' Shuggy. He's one for the Bar-L for sure.'

They had reached the relative safety of Craigiebank Road and all four boys trudged the final hundred yards to the tenement where the Duntocher contingent lived. Somewhat crestfallen, they stood by the close entrance, leaning against the wall.

'Hey! Things are lookin' up,' declared Danny. 'I've still got the Saltnshake crisps. I stuck them in my cagoule pocket when we legged it.'

He opened the packet, ripped the top edge off the wee blue bag and sprinkled the salt over the crisps. They took two crisps each and enjoyed the savoury crunchiness of the moment.

'Hi Charlie,' a sweet little voice rang out through the cool night air. From the black intestine of the close, the tiny wee figure of Inch High appeared.

'Hi Inch,' murmured Charlie.

'How was your bevvy? Did you get banjoed an' was it dead good?

'Aye, it was braw, hen. Just braw.'

Although she was staring at Charlie, he knew exactly where she was looking.

'Can I get a crisp? I love they Saltnshake ones.'

She licked her lips, her tongue inadvertently catching a bit of snot.

Danny handed the crisp poke to Charlie who looked into its salty depths.

'Aye, there's one left. You can have it, wee one. As someone once said, you should always save the best 'til last, eh Danny boy?'

4

AMABAM

'Repeat after me: *amabam, amabas, amabat, amabamus, amabatus, amabant.*'

Thirty voices droned in unison.

'*Amabam, amabas, amabat, amabamus, amabatus, amabant.*'

'Louder this time, with some enthusiasm.'

The volume went up, the delivery with increased gusto.

'*Amabam, amabas, amabat, amabamus, amabatus, amabant.*'

'Right, on your feet this time and even louder.'

A scraping of chairs on hard linoleum, a clearing of throats.

'*AMABAM, AMABAS, AMABAT, AMABAMUS, AMABATUS, AMABANT.*'

Mr Clooney, the Latin teacher, was not one to be trifled with. He hadn't been given the nickname Clooney the Looney for nothing. If you refused to enter into the delights of verb declension in his class with enough keenness and energy, he would not hesitate in reaching into the top drawer of his desk to pull out his belt, a nasty looking black tawse called *The Beast*, a weapon that struck fear into the hearts of even the hardiest of recalcitrants. Having a fundamentalist faith in Holy Mother Church just seemed to intensify his zealous pursuit of teaching the one and only language that truly mattered. To Clooney, Latin was not dead, merely in hibernation, and he was one of the disciples that would bring it back to its former glory. Every lesson would start with a recitation of one *Pater Noster* and ten *Ave Marias*, every pupil knowing every word of each prayer by heart. Conveniently forgetting such things as slavery and gladiatorial combat, Clooney the Looney firmly believed that the Roman Empire was the apotheosis of human civilisation. He also frequently quoted the Roman poet Juvenal's most famous phrase *'Mens sana in corpore sano'* — a healthy mind in a healthy body. Hence the regular use of the imperative 'Stand up!' when memorising vocabulary, his conviction being that the blood flowing round the circulatory system would better serve the brain if pupils were not so sedentary. However, his *pars de resistentiam* (he would never have used *piece de resistance*, French being a thoroughly decadent language) was his use of sound and fury when declining verbs. Wherever the stress lay on the polysyllabic words, he would thump his fist into the blackboard:

'*amaBAM, amaBAS, amaBAT, amaBAMus, amaBATus, amaBANT*'

The whole classroom shook, the windows rattled and the pupils quivered with fear at the pugilistic power exerted on the poor blackboard, all wondering what it would be like to be on the receiving end of one of those punches. The irony of the threat of violence being used to decline the imperfect tense of the verb 'to love' was completely lost on Clooney, irony being a concept alien to his absolutist view of the world.

'Right, turn to page 48 in *'Ecce Romani'* and do the exercises on the imperfect tense. Once you've finished that, we'll look at the future tense of *Amare*. I'll give you 15 minutes to complete the exercise.'

The class shuffled books, jotters, pens and pencils around their desks and settled down to silent study. Danny O'Connell was sitting beside Bob McFadden in this class, Latin being a subject that the ever-pragmatic Charlie Harkness had ditched as soon as he hit S3 ('It's broon breid – whit's the point 'o' that?'). McFadden – or McFud as he was commonly known – was a curious little gremlin-like creature, humphy-backed and somewhat saturnine in nature. His parents had sent him to a priest boarding school seminary in the north of Scotland when he was in S1, a destination many west of Scotland boys had been sent to in the 60s and 70s, their parents believing it was the next best thing to a private education without having to pay for it, the Faustian pact of handing one's first-born's soul over to the church a mere minor detail in the transaction. However, the promise of a lifetime of fulfilment - spreading the gospel and enforced celibacy - did not sit well with young Bob and, after two years of kicking against the system and much weeping and gnashing of teeth, he returned to Clydebank, if not broken, then certainly damaged.

Not many enjoyed the company of Bob, hence the nickname McFud. He had the reputation of being a bit odd but Danny O'Connell thought everyone was a bit odd – the world he had experienced so far seemed to be populated with weirdos and freaks – so he tended to reserve judgment. Danny was, therefore, pretty relaxed about sitting next to McFadden in the Latin class. There was even an added advantage of being his partner – Bob had been drummed thoroughly in the finer points of Latin in the seminary, so he knew all the answers. In a matter of minutes, they had completed the exercise.

Bob reached into his schoolbag and pulled out a little sketch book, his pride and joy. Whenever there was a lull in the academic proceedings he would scribble furiously on the pad. Danny was one of the few people Bob showed his scribblings to and, to be fair, O'Connell acknowledged that the boy had talent.

The only problem was that the externalisation of what was going on in McFadden's mind straddled the border between the grotesque and the aberrant. He had been working on a 'special' project the last few months, a series of sketches on the theme of torture. Most of these had been derivative stuff – images of medieval torture probably taken from his studying of the Inquisition the previous year (the Jesuits, as always, were very thorough). Bodies on racks, thumbscrews, Judas cradles, waterboarding – he merrily scribbled away, happy as the day was long. However, today, he seemed particularly animated.

'Hey, Danny,' he whispered.

Danny was busy with the important task of cleaning out the wax from his ear with the inside of a Bic pen, always a strangely satisfying sensation.

'Uh?' grunted Danny.

'I think I'm on tae somethin' noo.'

'Aye, whit's that?'

'Well, I'm fed up wi' drawing other people's tortures so I thought I'd make up my own.'

'Aye, well that's interestin'.' Danny replied, uncertain how much enthusiasm he should show for this turn of events.

'Do you want tae see?'

Now, Danny, in all truth, was none too keen about this idea but seeing as McFadden was honouring him with a sneaky-peak at his artistic brilliance, he thought he'd better go with the flow.

'Right, so I had this idea last night that a great torture would be if you took aw the bones oot a somebody you dinnae like and then poke them wi' a knife and make them run. It'd be dead funny. Their arms and legs would go flyin' aboot aw oe'r the place and they'd keep floppin' aroon like a…'

Bob paused trying to find an appropriate simile.

'…like a floppy thing. Whit d'yae think?'

Danny looked at the sketch pad and, sure enough, there, in charcoal no less, was a series of sketches, in cartoon format, showing a narrative of, firstly, skeletal extraction and then, secondly, a curious depiction of a masked figure prodding and poking flaccid flesh, limp arms and legs wibbling and wobbling across the page.

'Aye, that's really, ehh... imaginative, Bob. It's pure dead brilliant whit goes on in your noggin', so it is. Who woulda thought o' that, eh?'

'Glad you like it, Danny. I think I'll do somethin' wi' ... eyes next.'

Bob's own dark brown eyes shone with artistic invention as he leaned over the desk, covered the sketch pad with his arm, and started to scribble.

Danny meanwhile looked about the classroom, glad to be free from the clutches of McFud's febrile mind. Despite the fear that Clooney engendered in the minds of S3 Latin pupils, O'Connell liked this class. He loved the hush of productiveness that enveloped the room, a hush that signalled order and structure in a seemingly confused and jumbled world. In other subjects, there was always an underlying tension in the air, an almost tangible friction between adult tyranny and adolescent bloody-mindedness. The Latin teacher, despite his idiosyncrasies, always seemed to strike the right balance. Danny's fellow students actually learned stuff here and, despite the rote learning nature of Clooney's pedagogy, it was hugely effective. He stared at the heads bent over the jotters and textbooks, thirty minds collectively soaking in knowledge.

But wait. Thirty minds? Make that 29. On the other side of the classroom by the window, a pretty female face was staring across the room in his direction. In fact, Danny got the distinct impression she was staring at him. He looked to the side of him, just to check it wasn't McFud she was looking at but he was lost in his own little world of sketching ocular mutilation. Danny glanced back at her, just to make sure that he wasn't imagining it. Sure enough, she was still gazing at him, this time with the slightest hint of a coquettish smile. This was Catherine Mathieson, one of the prettiest girls in the year, and Catherine Mathieson was eyeing him up.

'Oh boy... Oh boy, oh boy, oh boy,' thought Danny to himself. 'Keep calm. Act cool.'

O'Connell did not have the smallest inkling of how to act cool but he thought by saying it to himself, it might help. There were lads in his year group that had an aura of maturity about them when they conversed with girls, and he was slightly in awe of the relaxed easy manner they had around those of the opposite sex. No girl had ever shown the remotest interest in him since moving to secondary school. He remembered that he had had a wee crush on Rosemary Mullen back in Primary 3, and she had expressed a reciprocal attachment to him, but her parents had moved to England and the great romance had been throttled at birth. More recently, however, the allure of the female form had taken up much conversation time with Charlie, Martin and Tony, most of it focusing on the burgeoning blossoming of girls' chests, the bigger the breasts the more attractive the girl. However, the opening salvos of actual dialogue between any of these boys and any willing girl had not taken place. The risks were too high.

Now, suddenly, Catherine's come-hither look was a game changer. He thought that the best strategy would be to simply copy what she was doing. He would smile back at her. Danny's pimply face cracked into a rictus. 'Christ almighty – how difficult is it to smile naturally,' he thought to himself. He felt that his opening signal of intent was more of a creepy leer but, lo and behold, she smiled again, this time with coy embarrassment. Looking down at her jotter, doodling on the page, Catherine then slowly raised her head and, looking at him again, put the tip of the little rubber at the end of her pencil gently against her lips.

'Oh boy, oh boy, oh boy, oh boy.'

Something Darwinian stirred within Danny's loins. He shifted uncomfortably in his seat and tried to re-arrange the anatomical furniture but it was no use. Cupid's arrow had hit him below the belt. The gusset of his polyester charcoal trousers was being stretched to breaking point.

'Right, we're going to look at the future tense of *Amare*, now,' bellowed Clooney, 'so if you turn to page 50.'

Danny was somewhat relieved that the world of academia had re-asserted itself – however, his big predicament had not resolved itself, the big predicament having a mind of its own.

'OK, let's have someone recite the future tense of 'To Love.'

Danny muttered to himself, 'Please, no, no, no.'

'O'Connell. On your feet.'

A whimper emanated from Danny's anguished mouth. This was worse than any torture that McFadden's warped mind could conjure up.

'Please, sir can I no' recite it sitting doon? I've got a bit o'a sore... back.'

'Nonsense, boy, on your feet. The Romans didn't build an empire sitting on their backside.'

Danny stuck his hands in his pockets and tried re-arranging the alignment of things but that just seemed to make matters worse. He pushed the chair back with a wriggle of his buttocks then slowly stood up, his comportment having a passing resemblance to The Hunchback of Notre Dame.

'Get your hands out of your pockets and stand up straight. You need some blood rushing round your system boy.'

Danny knew exactly where his blood was rushing to and he really didn't want the world to know it. Suddenly, inspired, he took his hands out of his pockets, quickly stood up straight and rattled out the declension:

'*Amambampot,   amabiscuit,   amabitofafud,   amablootered, amabladdered, amabunt.*'

He just as quickly sat down again. Stoney silence. The pupils themselves were too scared to breathe.

Clooney the Looney, for the first time in living memory, was temporarily lost for words. He walked over to O'Connell's desk and towered over him.

'Have you taken leave of your senses, boy?'

Danny stared at the varnished desk, clutching the edges of it, shoulders hunched. Some wag had scraped into its surface the message, 'Beam me up, Scottie.' He smiled.

'Do you find this funny, O'Connell?'

'No, sir.'

Clooney marched back to the front of the class, opened the top drawer of his desk and brought out *The Beast*.

The next few minutes were a bit of a blur for Danny but while the inevitable happened, he comforted himself with the knowledge that, due to his quick thinking, he had avoided public humiliation. His big predicament had quickly resolved itself at the first sight of *The Beast* and he accepted his punishment with a mixture of gratitude and pride. After all, as Clooney delivered the sixth blow on his stinging hands, in his peripheral vision, he was sure that Catherine Mathieson was, once again, smiling at him.

5

THE SPALDING DOT

anny stared at the long plastic cylinder riveted at a 45-degree angle to the side of the pebble-dashed cabin that served as a starter's hut. There was a nervous fluttering in his stomach as he realised that his old, scuffed Dunlop 65 was the next ball out of the tube, the time-honoured method for establishing order of play, and he would be standing on the tee in the next few minutes, playing golf on a proper golf course for the first time in his life.

This was Dalmuir Municipal Park, a public course owned and run by the council and, on this sunny Saturday morning, for the princely sum of 10p, a junior could play the eighteen holes and dream of being the next Jack Nicklaus or Tom Watson. Scotland, as a nation, had always prided itself in being The Home of Golf but this was no abstract concept, the game being hard-wired into the collective psyche, the sport accessible to all classes of society. Aside from private courses spanning the length and breadth of the country, there was a network of public courses that allowed the working-class man (and the occasional woman) to spend his or her leisure time in this healthy pursuit. So, for a nominal fee, golfers of every shape and ability would merrily chase wee white balls across handsome landscapes every weekend, come rain, hail or shine. Golf in many ways encapsulated the founding principles of the French Republic – Liberty, Equality, Fraternity – and, away from the divisive tribal nature of Scottish football, golf, like fishing, was a force for good and, generally speaking, brought Scots together rather than forced them apart.

The reason why Danny had walked four miles from Faifley, via Duntocher, to stand anxiously at the gate to the first tee, was his friend, Charlie. He had persuaded Danny to join him on his own weekly round of golf, a ritual he had started when he was merely ten years old. Over the last four years, Harkness had fallen in love with the game, the sport providing him simultaneously with an escape from the world of academia and also an identity. Through practice, perseverance and a gift for eye-to-hand co-ordination, Charlie had developed into a prodigious talent. This, he knew, was what defined him. It is what gave him self-belief. It is what gave him the gallus confidence to look the world in the eye and say, 'I'm as good as you, perhaps even better.'

Danny, on the other hand, was not a sporting prodigy. He wasn't completely haun'less, as they say, but whenever an impromptu game of footie was arranged at break time in school and teams were to be selected, he was one of the last to be chosen. With the destination for most adolescent Catholic boys being a football stadium in the East End of Glasgow on a Saturday afternoon, Charlie realised that the pool of sporting excellence available to him was decidedly shallow and although he wasn't quite dredging the bottom, Danny would provide him with company, if nothing else. Danny had played pitch and putt with two hired clubs on holiday in Millport the previous summer, so he was not unfamiliar with the basic concepts of golf. In recognition of this step-up in scale, however, Danny's dad had managed to dig out from the loft, an old half set of hickory shafted clubs that his own father had bequeathed to him, a set so ancient that Old Tom Morris would have looked askance at them. Picking up his ball from the tube, Danny slung his moth-eaten tattered canvas bag on his shoulder and descended the steps to the first tee.

'What the hell are those?' bellowed Charlie, staring at Danny's bag of scrap iron.

'They're my dad's clubs... well actually, they're my grandad's clubs... well, actually, they could be my great grandad's clubs. They're probably worth somethin', y'know. Collector's items - so don't you go slagging them off, ya golfing snob, ye.'

'Aye, bin man's collection.'

Charlie pulled Danny's driver out of the bag and examined it.

'I think this one's got woodworm.'

'Just you worry aboot your own game, aw right, Charlie.'

Danny looked at Charlie's bag, a gleaming black and white Ben Hogan job, with a full set of gleaming Wilson Staff woods and blades. Charlie's parents had recognised their son's talent and passion from the very start, his dad being a keen golfer himself, and they had made not inconsiderable financial sacrifices to give him a competitive edge.

'They look awful shiny,' remarked Danny. 'Better watch ye don't scuff them. My clubs, on the other hand, have got character. At least mine have that lived-in look.'

'Aye, like an old tramp on the El D. Come on, the starter's given us the thumbs up.'

Charlie strode onto the junior tee box as if he was king of all he surveyed. Not only did he have the bag and the clubs, he also had dark green tartan troos and a pair of black and white shoes, spat-like, squeaky clean. Danny trudged behind him, wearing his trademark red cagoul, polyester charcoal trousers and a pair of white sannies.

'You got enough golf balls?' enquired Charlie.

'Don't you worry aboot me, Charlie boy,' replied Danny, though he glanced rather nervously into the front pouch of his bag. There was only one scabby Penfold Ace sitting forlornly at the bottom of the pouch and, apart from the Dunlop 65 in his hand, that was it.

'Ok, I'll show you the way,' announced Charlie. 'This is a par 4, so you're meant tae do this in four shots.'

'I know whit par 4 means. I didnae come up the Clyde in a banana boat.'

'Just trying tae help.'

Charlie pulled his driver out of the bag, took a ball out of his pocket, then teed it up. He took a couple of practice swings then addressed the Spalding Dot with a fearsome concentration that somewhat intimidated Danny, such was its intensity. Charlie then swung through the ball with grace, elegance and power. He sent the projectile fizzing through the air with such speed that Danny lost sight of it. A round of applause burst forth from the golfers waiting at the starter's box.

'Fine shot, Charlie... Belter... He's a talent, that one... On yersel' Charlie boy...'

'That's nearly on the green,' announced Charlie smugly, 'That's how tae do it, Danny son. You're on an elevated tee here so you can see everything. Avoid the trees and bushes on the right and the burn on the left - just hit it doon the middle. Dead easy.'

Danny, all of a sudden, felt all eyes were upon him. He wasn't imagining it. The regulars at Dalmuir knew Charlie and recognised a golfer when they saw one. If Charlie had a new golfing buddy, he must be pretty handy himself. Danny reached into his pocket and brought out an old wooden tee, chipped and half-broken. He stuck it in the ground and attempted to place his ball on it. For some inexplicable reason, his hand was shaking.

'Christ, catch a grip, Danny,' he said to himself.

The ball toppled off its perch. He bent down again and repositioned it. Again it fell off.

'I think my tee's knackered,' said Danny.

'Have you only got one?' enquired Charlie, a hint of impatience creeping into the tone of his voice.

'Aye. Didnae think I'd need more than one.'

'Here. Take a couple o' these.'

'I'll pay you back for them.'

'Just get a move on, Danny. The natives are gettin' restless back there.'

'Aye righty-ho. Here we go.'

Having teed it up, he bent over and extracted the driver from the bag. He then addressed the ball the way Charlie had done a couple of minutes earlier. The first thing he noticed was how long the driver felt. This wasn't anything like pitch and putt. He felt miles away from it. Still, he was here to play golf and golf he would play. He drew the club back, then flung himself at the Dunlop 65, arms, hips, legs, almost every part of his anatomy being launched at the little white sphere. His head whipped upwards, eyes seeking any sign of parabolic flight down the fairway.

'Where'd it go?' enquired a somewhat bemused Danny.

Charlie glowered at him with a look of total and utter disdain. He pointed at the ground in front of Danny. He looked down and, there, sitting on the tee, was the Dunlop 65, untouched and unmoved.

'Aye. OK. That was my practice swing, Charlie. That didnae count. Here we go.'

'Come on, Danny,' he exhorted to himself, 'How hard can it be tae hit a stationary ball. Let's knock this wee white shite oot the park.'

A swing. A swoosh of air. Time stood still and so did the ball.

Another and another and another, each swish getting faster and faster.

Suddenly, Danny felt a reverberation through the shaft of the club and a heard a 'clonk'. The ball squirted forward and disappeared off its elevated position, bobbling along the ground and coming to rest about 40 yards away. Unfortunately, the 'clonk' was not the only sound that was heard. At the same time as 'Clonk', there was 'Crack', then a noise that had a passing resemblance to the whirring of helicopter blades. The head of Danny's driver had become detached from the shaft and, unlike the ball, was airborne, its whipped binding unravelling and uncoiling like a fishing line cast from a rod. The wooden clubhead disappeared over the edge of the tee.

A momentary hush descended. Then laughter erupted followed by thunderous applause, far louder than the polite and appreciative clapping that Charlie's drive had engendered.

Danny turned and waved to the assembled audience behind him, Charlie shaking his head in bamboozled bewilderment.

'Holy crap,' announced Danny, 'I don't think that's supposed tae happen,' as he turned and, picking up the unravelled black thread, reeled in the rogue driver head. 'I think this might be buggered, Charlie,' he reasoned as he showed him the decapitated golf club, his half set now indubitably depleted by one.

'Look, just shove it in the bag, grab your 7 iron and belt it doon the fairway. The whole course is gonnae back up cos o' you. You're a pure riddy, you are.'

'Aw right, haud yer whisht. It's only a game,' countered Danny as he trudged down the fairway, slashing at the ball with his seven iron, advancing it only a few yards at a time. He carried his bag in his right hand, not bothering to sling it over his shoulder as it seemed too much of an effort between one shot and the next.

'Only a game! Only a game! Don't talk mince, ya big

ignoramus. This is the only game worth talkin' aboot, the game I love. It's a game o' skill, o' power an' touch an' feel and strategy an' control an' it's aw aboot just you, the ball and the course. It's a test o' character, so it is. Ye cannae blame anyone but yirsel' if things go wrong. It's the best game in the world. So don't gie me any o' that *only a game* shite.'

While Charlie was extolling the virtues of his beloved sport, Danny realised the green was now about 150 yards away. There was a white ball just a few yards short of it, the clear manifestation of his friend's undoubted prowess. He thought maybe this time he could fire it towards the hole, onto the putting surface, maybe even putt it in one, such is the eternal optimism of the hacker. However, once again he topped the ball a mere 10 yards.

'Christ, you're like a caveman wi' a club, Danny. Keep yer heid doon.'

And then a strange thing happened.

Just as Danny was about to duff his next shot, he looked up. To the rear of the green was a large beech hedge, at least six feet in height, a demarcation line between the first hole and the second. Suddenly, a small scurrying figure wearing denim trousers and a blue anorak, appeared from a gap in the hedge. It scuttled across the first green, ran over to Charlie's ball, picked it up and disappeared back behind the hedge.

'Eh, Charlie? Is that supposed tae happen?'

Charlie, his concentration totally focused on fixing the golfing abomination that was Danny's swing, had missed the brazen daylight robbery.

'Naw. You're no' supposed tae top it like that. I said that you're lifting yer heid. Try watching the ball and not anticipatin' the shot.'

'I think you should maybe watch yer own baw and do a bit o' anticipatin' yersel'. Someone's half-inched it.'

'What?' cried Charlie, scanning the front of the green for signs of his Spalding Dot.

'That's a brand new ball. What the hell happened?'

'Well, a wee chap came oot from behind that hedge, ran across the green and whipped yer Balding Spot.'

'It's called a Spalding Dot, ya moron.'

'Well, you'll have tae call it the Vanishing Dot. That wee guy's got it noo.'

'I don't believe it. What sort o' a place is this, random people just runnin' aboot knickin' yer golf balls.'

'Did you no' say it's all aboot *just you, the ball and the course?* You forgot tae mention wee shites hidin' behind hedges gettin' in the way.'

'Shut it Danny. This is not how the game is supposed to be played. I mean Jack Nicklaus doesnae have tae put up wi' this sort o' crap. How am I supposed tae become a top-class golfer under these conditions? Where's the polis when ye need them?'

'And, did you no' also say *Ye cannae blame anyone but yirsel' if things go wrong?*'

Charlie looked as if he was going to take out his 5 iron and brain Danny with it but he shook his head, muttering profanities, then marched up to the edge of the green, dropping a new ball on the fringe. Sensing that he should maybe remain silent for the next couple of minutes, Danny, now well into double figures, carried on knocking his ball ever closer to the green. Charlie laid his clubs on the ground, pulled out his putter and holed out in two, Danny at least double that.

'I think that was 21.'

'Christ,' muttered Charlie.

'That's me one up.'

'Whit d'ye mean?'

'Well, you lost a ball so that means I win the hole. Is that no' how it works?

Charlie was on the verge of apoplectic implosion when suddenly a shrill nasally voice pierced the air.

'Hey, dae ye want tae buy a golf ball, mister?'

A scrawny hobgoblin wearing denim trousers and a blue anorak had stepped out from behind the hedge. The kid looked no more seven years old. Charlie and Danny moved towards him.

'That's the one that knicked yer ball, Charlie,' whispered Danny.

Charlie, simmering anger bubbling to boiling point, strode menacingly towards the little gremlin.

'Aye. Aw' right, sonny, let's see whit ye've got.'

The three of them stepped behind the hedge.

A grubby hand held out the ball.

'That's my Spalding Dot, ya wee shite. My brand new Spalding Dot. You just knicked it aff the fairway a couple o' minutes ago and I've got a witness as well. Tell him Danny.'

Danny, all of a sudden, was silent. Only the sound of rustling leaves could be heard as the wind blew through the branches of the hedge.

'I said, *Tell him, Danny.*'

'Eh, Charlie, check it out behind you.'

Charlie turned and, standing behind him was the biggest man he had ever seen. He must have been pushing 7 feet and he had shoulders that blocked out the sun.

'Are you callin' my son a tea leaf?'

Charlie gulped. The giant bear took the ball from the little boy's hand, held it up in front of Charlie's face - and growled.

'I said - are you callin' my son a tea leaf?'

Charlie shook his head, his throat suffering from a most peculiar constriction. Son of the giant slipped silently around the side of the hedge.

'Well, if yer no callin' my boy a tea leaf, then you'd maybe like tae buy his golf ball, eh? 10p an' it's all yours.'

'B... b... but...' stuttered Harkness, a raging sense of injustice coursing through him.

One giant fist grabbed Charlie's shirt, one huge face stooped to his eye-level.

'10... pence... and... it's... yours.'

Each syllable was laden with jeopardy. The ogre let go of him. With trembling hands, Charlie reached into his pockets, extracted 10p and handed it over.

'One brand new Spalding Dot, all for you, sonny. A bargain indeed.'

He dropped the ball into Charlie's hand, wandered down the track, then disappeared around the corner.

'Does this happen every week, Charlie?' asked Danny, once he felt it was safe to breathe again.

'Naw – I've never seen them before. They must be frae Glasgow. Bankies wouldnae behave like that. Come on. Let's get on with the round. Put it doon to experience.'

They returned to the green to pick up their clubs but there was only one bag sitting by the side of the green – and it wasn't Charlie's.

'Where the hell's ma bag?' cried Charlie.

His shiny Wilson staff clubs in their shiny Ben Hogan bag had gone. He ran to the gap in the hedge and down the track to the corner where he had last seen the Glaswegian Goliath– but there was no one on the horizon, the woods and the hilly terrain facilitating a quick get-away...

The walk back to Duntocher was funereal. Stoicism was always a state of mind that was valued highly in the West coast of Scotland but Charlie was finding it hard to choke back the tears. His parents' most meaningful birthday present to him, his treasured clubs, the clubs that allowed him to express himself without having to use words or paint pictures, had been cruelly snatched away. In the years to come, there would be other sets of clubs, tournaments that would be won, trophies that would be held aloft but, for now, the raw pain of loss and anger was overwhelming.

Danny did not say much, sensing that any expression of sympathy would only scratch the surface of Charlie's anguish and heartache. As he slogged silently up the hill on the long way home, his old scabby canvas bag with its load of broken and nearly broken sticks on his shoulders, he just knew that walking step by step beside his friend would be enough.

ROMEO, ROMEO...

And we sang shang-a-lang
And we ran with the gang
Doin' doo-op-dooby-doo-i
We were all in the news
With our blue suede shoes
And dancin' the night away.
Yeah, we sang shang-a-lang
And we ran with the gang
Doin' doo-op-dooby-doo-i
With the juke box playin'
And everybody sayin'
That music like ours couldn't die.

The day before the October holiday at Danny's school was always an interesting display of time-wasting on the part of the teachers. Most of them just wished the minutes would whistle by so that they could all head to the local boozer as a cohort and exorcise the term's demons with a skinful of booze, the catharsis demanding a minimum of six pints and six shorts. Some didn't even bother to wait until 3.45pm, preferring to knock back a few pints at lunchtime, then sleep it off in the final two periods of the afternoon. Woe-betide any pupil that stirred Gleeson from his slumbers in the Maths class, the pupils preferring to keep their heads down playing Noughts and Crosses, Hangman or Battleships in their jotters.

However, there was one teacher who actually tried to do something meaningful with the kids, something a little bit different on the final day. He was Mr Ferry, a conscientious music teacher who doubled-up as Danny and Charlie's form master. The class before Friday morning break was weekly form time, ordinarily given over to a little bit of RE (Religious Education) or a time spent pointlessly reinforcing the seemingly ever-expanding list of school rules. However, Ferry always set aside this particular period on the last day of term to allow his pupils to bring in their own vinyl records and seven or eight singles would then be played – on one condition: the pupil had to stand up and articulate at least one reason why they liked that particular song. It was a win-win situation for everyone – the kids could chill out while listening to music; the teacher had a happy class and he was able to salve his conscience by convincing himself that pupils justifying their aesthetic tastes was both educational and character building.

Thus, the final bars of 'Shang-a-Lang' rang round the walls of the music room, walls adorned with the posters of stern Beethovens and Mozarts and Schuberts and Haydns. This particular song was the choice of Bridgette Mahoney, a short dumpy little lassie in pig tails and NHS black rimmed specs. The other girls in the class had murmured their approval at her selection and sixteen female heads had bobbed up and down, feet tapping in time to the beat, all the way through the song. The Bay City Rollers were still swoon-worthy for S3 girls. The majority of the boys liked these guys as well, their kitsch Scottishness pandering to their sense of national identity, but they would never admit this openly, a boy band maybe not macho enough for your average red-blooded adolescent Scot. The Rolling Stones, The Who, even The Eagles were within the spectrum of male acceptability and normality - anything going much beyond these musical spheres left oneself open to accusations of dubious taste and questionable sexuality.

'So, Bridgette, what is it that you like about 'Shang-a-Lang?' enquired Mr Ferry once the twanging guitar chords had drifted into the ether.

'I just 'hink Woodie's drop dead gorgeous, Mr Ferry.'

The other girls purred their approval of Mahoney's in-depth analysis of her musical taste.

'Come, come, Bridgette, I'm sure we can go a bit deeper than that as far as your liking of his music is concerned. Can you give me more detail?'

Bridgette furrowed her brow, deep in concentration.

'Aw right, sir. It's that photie of him topless, with the wee red tartan scarf aroon' his neck. I nearly passed oot when I saw that, so I did.'

Collective purring morphed into collective cooing as the girls pictured this vision of loveliness. The boys in the class looked on at these strange creatures and the world that they inhabited. Like the green alien woman that Captain Kirk had kissed in 'Star Trek', they were both attracted and repelled at what they saw.

'OK, Bridgette, I suppose that is analysis of a sort. Thank you. Just before we choose the next song, I hope you'll indulge my curiosity. Is there anyone in here who didn't like the song?'

A stony silence. All the boys knew that putting a hand up to denigrate the blessed Rollers was tantamount to ruining any chance of scoring with any girl at any time from now until they died.

All the boys, it would appear, except one.

Danny O'Connell slowly raised his hand in the air, his antennae telling him that this was probably not the smartest thing he was ever going to do but his disdain for the warbling trash that he'd just heard had over-ruled his head.

'Oh, Danny. That's very brave of you to put up your hand. Could you let me know why you don't like the song?'

'Well, where dae I begin, sir. I mean, first of aw the lyrics. Whit sort o' nonsense is *doo-op-dooby-doo-i*? Whit's aw that aboot? Anythin' wi' a *dooby-doo* in it should be throttled at birth. And don't get me started oan the music. I thought the Status Quo's book o' chords was the smallest book in the world but I stand corrected – it's the Bay City Rollers' teeny-weeny wee teeny miniscule book o'chords. And as for their musicianship, sir. The drummer sounds as if he's a big ape wi' two sticks and my wee dug's got better manual dexterity on a guitar than Stuart 'Woody' Wood. They're pure unadulterated pi... piffle, sir.'

The music teacher smiled, the girls scowled with barely concealed malevolence and the boys gawped in awed silence. O'Connell, having got that off his chest, sat back feeling mightily good about himself. Charlie leaned across the desk and whispered, 'Bloody hell, Danny. That was awesome.'

'OK, O'Connell. Since you obviously have opinions about music, perhaps we should choose your song next.'

The class groaned but Danny had the bit between his teeth. He handed Ferry an LP and instructed:

'Final movement. Beethoven's 9th – The Choral Symphony. Greatest piece o' music ever written. Broke all the rules. Wrote it for the universal brotherhood of Man. Most people know it as 'Ode tae Joy.' The film 'Clockwork Orange' used it for a lot o' the scenes – not that I've ever seen it, obviously. But this is proper music, sir.'

'Indeed it is, O'Connell. Indeed it is.'

For the next eighteen minutes, it has to be said, the Ode to Joy did not engender much in the way of universal brotherhood or, indeed, sisterhood. After five minutes there was a great deal of shuffling of feet; after ten minutes many of the girls had put their hands over their ears; after fifteen, the lassies looked sideways at him with barely concealed hostility and venom. By the end, if Ferry had not been in the class, O'Connell would have been lynched. As chance would have it, the bell rang just at the moment where there was a strong stench of rebellion in the air.

'O'Connell – ya freak ye... Ya waste o'space... There's a village missin' an idiot...' were some of the more benign declarations of support for Danny as they left the music room and shuffled along the corridor. As they filtered outside into the playground, Charlie walked along beside his buddy.

'Ach, just ignore that lot. You were right. Bay City Rollers are crap. I wish I had backed you up, by the way. I liked aw that stuff aboot universal brotherhood an' aw that. Music should be more than silly wee love songs. You know I'm intae Genesis and Emerson, Lake and Palmer and prog rock. I cannae be daein wi' aw that pop shite.'

Charlie also appreciated that Danny was no mean musician. His mother, scrimping and saving and sacrificing for years, had sent him to piano lessons when he was only seven and he was now at Grade 8 level. Just as Charlie could hit a golf ball with consummate ease, Danny could rattle off a piano sonata *con brio*. The rest of the school acknowledged this, giving him the nickname Mozart. However, it dawned on him that enforcing his esoteric musical tastes on the general populace had been a step too far.

'I think I might've pushed it a bit there wi' Beethoven's 9th, Charlie. I mean, did ye see the lassies – I thought they were gonnae pure molocate me.'

'Aye, I think ye might have blown yer chances o' findin' a burd this side o' paradise.'

'Ehhh, well... That's where I think ye might be wrong.'

'Whit dae ye mean?'

'Can you keep a secret?'

'Aye, course I can.'

'I mean really keep a secret.'

'I said I can. Whit's aw this aboot?'

'Swear on your mother's grave.'

'Aye, swear on my mother's grave.'

'I think Catherine Mathieson fancies me.'

'Get away.'

'Naw, I mean it.'

'How d'ye know?'

'Well, ye know how I got six o' the belt frae Clooney the Looney the ither day...'

'Aye, I heard that. Whit wis that for?'

Danny hesitated, weighing up the pros and cons of going into the gory details of his Big Predicament. He decided to err on the side of caution.

'Long story - but just before I got belted she was eyeing me up in class. She couldnae stop looking at me. I'm tellin' ye, she fancies me somethin' rotten.'

'She's awright as well. I wouldnae say naw.'

'Piss off, Charlie. I saw her first. I've got dibs on her.'

'Aw right. Keep yer knickers oan. So, whit ye gonnae dae aboot it?'

Danny frowned. This was obviously the snag he had hit.

'Ehhh. I don't really know. Never had a burd interested in me. Whit would you do?'

Now, Charlie had always given the impression to Danny that he was a Man of the World but, when push came to shove, he was in exactly the same bottom division of cluelessness as his pal. Just at that point the bell rang for the start of period 4. The boys were heading off to separate subjects, Danny to History, Charlie to Physics, both double periods.

'To be continued, Danny me boy. I will give you my pearls of wisdom at lunchtime.'

'OK, Charlie... and Charlie?'

'Eh?'

'Top secret. Not a word tae nobody, right?'

'Aye, nae bother. See ye later, big man.'

For the next two periods, Danny sat in the History class, his mind not fully focused on the intricacies of The Russian Revolution. He didn't really give a tuppeny curse whether the White Bolsheviks or the Red Bolsheviks or the Pink with Blue Polka Dot Bolsheviks were winning the battle for supremacy. His thoughts kept drifting to the pretty face of Catherine Mathieson, his one true love. What was Charlie's advice going to be? What should be Danny's opening line? Would he go for a quick quip or fawning flattery? Was the way to a woman's heart through humour or romance? But above all else, what was he going to do about his plukes? She had never really seen him up close and personal so this could be a bit of a problem. She might sprint for the hills when she clapped eyes on his craterous kisser. He vowed there and then to be abstemious when it came to the crisps and the chocolate and the Creamola Foam. There was going to be a new Danny, a new dawn, a new, improved O'Connell, pluke-free – a babe magnet but not just any old babe – a Catherine Mathieson babe magnet.

Time dragged by but eventually the clock pushed the minute hand to 12.30pm and the bell rang. Danny packed up his books and headed for the spot just behind the PE block where he and Charlie would always meet before heading off to the City Bakeries to buy a pie, a sausage roll or a bridie, such was the smorgasbord of savoury delights on offer in the West of Scotland – and on a good day you could smother it all with a heap of baked beans.

Charlie was not there but standing in a little huddle was a group of S3 boys from the Physics class. They all turned and suddenly went on bended knee:

'Romeo, Romeo, Wherefoor art thou Romeo!'

Danny's heart skipped a beat. What was this?

'Heh, O'Connell, ya big fud. Whit's this ye fancy Catherine Mathieson?'

Danny's heart skipped two more beats.

Tommy Lang, one of the biggest and most intimidating hoodlums in S3, stepped forward, a leering grin spread across his ugly mug. Tommy was the black-market king in the school – anything you wanted, Tommy could get: cheap cigarettes, knocked off vodka, emergency supply of prophylactics and, of course, the much coveted and highly desirable scud mag.

'I don'know whit ye mean, Tommy.'

'Oh yes ye dae. A wee burdie told me ye've got the hots for Mathieson, that wee burdie bein' yer best mate Harkness. Sang like a canary when he foon oot there's a brand new scud mag in circulation. *Oh, Tommy, Tommy gie's the scud mag for the night an' I'll tell ye somehin' funny.* Dinnae realise it'd be that funny. You and Catherine Mathieson? Yer aff yer heid.'

'Naw Tommy, it's no like that...'

'Aye it is. Come oan. Let's go an' see whit she has tae say aboot it. Might even set ye up for a night o' rumpy-pumpy. Let's go lads.'

Tommy's henchmen grabbed Danny's collar, pinned his arms behind him and frogmarched him round to the front of the science block, the part of the playground where the S3 girls generally gathered. By the time Tommy and his gang had reached the front entrance to the block, a sizeable crowd had gathered behind him, word having spread that there was good theatre in the offing. Catherine was standing with two of her friends, just about to bite into a salmon paste sandwich.

Subtle as ever, Lang bellowed, 'Oi, Mathieson!'

Her mouth closed. She glanced nervously at her friends, then looked at the mangy mob in front of her, at the centre of which was the rather bedraggled figure of Danny O'Connell, his head lowered, a picture of crushed dejection and shame.

'O'Connell here says he wants intae yer knickers. Whit do ye say tae that? Fancy gie'in him wan?'

The young girl blushed and looked once more towards her chums for some sort of moral support but they averted their gaze and looked impassively at the ground.

'Well, Mathieson. Whit's it gonnae be? How can ye say no tae lover-boy here? I mean look at that face. How can ye no resist the pullin' powers o' Plukeyman here.'

The crowd guffawed with pitiless laughter, Lang's alliterative barb hitting the spot.

'I'd rather have my eyes poked oot wi' a blunt stick than go oot wi' Danny O'Connell,' declared Miss Mathieson who promptly turned and disappeared into the Science block, her two friends scurrying inside after her.

The crowd cheered. Lang leaned in close to Danny and whispered, 'Know yer place, O'Connell. Catherine Mathieson's no for the likes o' you. Now, sling yer hook.'

His cronies released their grip on Danny and, as he turned to go, Lang kicked him up the backside, the whack a visual, tactile and auditory full stop to the whole proceedings. The throng dispersed, well pleased with the little drama that had played out in front of them, a mini diversion from the humdrum tedium of school life.

Danny stood alone in front of the science building and stared morosely at the ground. He had never before noticed how many dried-up bits of chewing gum there were stuck to the tarmac, a veritable Milky Way of spent Wrigley's mastication, little blobs that had started off as sleek strips in shiny wrappers but had been ripped open, chewed up and, in the end, spat out. He wandered the perimeter of the school for the rest of lunchtime, preferring to be left alone, his appetite gone, his faith in humanity squashed.

By the cruellest twist of fate, the afternoon double period was Latin and it was purgatorial. He was well aware of the whisperings and the stifled giggles but what hurt the most was the fact that he could no longer look to his right and glance at what had been the object of his desire. He briefly wondered what she was feeling right now, whether she had just experienced a similar crushing of the soul but then he mentally swatted it aside for she was tarnished now. Mixed in with the stench of rejection, there was a whiff of betrayal as well.

Danny breathed a sigh of relief when the bell rang for the end of the day. He just wanted to go home, start the holiday and practise his beloved piano for a couple of hours, the intricacies of a Bach fugue perfect for reorientating the mind and cleansing the soul. As he walked through the school gates a familiar voice called to him.

'Danny! Wait up.'

'Piss aff, Charlie. We're finished.'

'Danny. I never thought he would dae that.'

Danny increased his stride length, desperate to create space between himself and his erstwhile friend.

'Aye well, mibbe ye should have thought a bit harder.'

Danny stopped and turned on him, tears glistening in his eyes.

'Christ, Charlie. Ye swore on yer mither's grave not tae tell anyone.'

'Aye well, my maw's no deid yet so, strictly speaking, that didnae count.'

Danny stepped towards him, his fist clenched, a vein throbbing in his temple. Charlie backed off, putting his hands up, palms out.

'Steady, big man, steady. Look, if it makes ye feel any better, it all went a bit tit's up for me as well. After Lang gave me the scud mag, I was in Techie Drawing an' Mr Donnelly spotted it in my bag. He confiscated it and gave me six o' the belt calling me a 'depraved reprobate', whitever that means. Tommy Lang's in that class as well and was right beelin' when he saw his magazine disappearing intae Donnelly's top drawer. He grabbed me straight after class and smacked me in the coupon and said I'd have tae pay tae replace this month's edition.'

Danny looked at Charlie's face and noticed a distinct swelling of the right eye, the first tell-tale signs of a real keecher.

'Serves ye right, ya fud. Maybe that'll teach ye.'

To be fair on Charlie, he had very quickly, and painfully, come to realise that maybe using the currency of his best friend's romantic secrets in exchange for soft porn was not his finest hour.

'Listen, Danny,' he said, looking pleadingly with his one good eye at O'Connell's now somewhat placated face, 'I'm sorry. I was bang oot o' order in daein' that tae ye. Are we good?'

Danny stared at him and, after a couple of moment's reflection, nodded. After all, weighing it up, he reckoned out of the fiasco that had been the day's events, having a bruised heart was marginally better than having a bruised face.

7

LUNCH WITH MOTHER

'Mum, can I get an Adidas T-shirt, please?'

'No.'

'But why not?'

'Firstly, they are too expensive and, secondly, every wee ned in the neighbourhood wears an Adidas T-shirt, just as every wee ned in the district rides a Chopper bike and every wee ned in the country has long hair. You are not going to become a wee ned, Daniel.'

'Aw, mum, please. It's my birthday coming up soon and that's all I really want.'

'Tell me this, Daniel. Does Charles Harkness own an Adidas T-shirt?'

This was a side-step shimmy worthy of Jimmy Johnstone. Danny, smelling danger, obfuscated.

'Maybe. I don't know. I can't rightly remember if he has one.'

This was not entirely untrue. Charlie, indeed, did not have one Adidas T-shirt. He had three: yellow with blue stripes, red with black stripes and green with white stripes. These were all secretly coveted by Danny, though, if truth be told, he desperately wanted a white with black stripes top. Own one of those and he would be cock of the north.

'Well, I presume it's the sort of wee neddish thing that Charles Harkness would wear. Just as I assume he watches Top of the Pops and all that goes with that.'

Danny's mum - a devout Catholic who attended mass more often than the parish priest - had a prejudice so irrational about 'Top of the Pops' that any mention of the programme would have a Pavlovian response of such intensity that Danny and his brother and sister would run for cover. She had read in the Scottish Sunday Express about some depraved phenomenon that was a regular feature on 'Top of the Pops' called Pan's People and how they were corrupting the souls of young men – and women – with their over-sexualised gyrations and lude pelvic thrusts. As far as she was concerned, this was the beginning of the end of civilisation, a descent into a dark, chaotic, amoral pit of Sodom and Gomorrah depth. The moral crusader of the time, Mary Whitehouse, was a libertarian in comparison to Mrs O'Connell. Indeed, anything to do with modern popular culture was treated with disdain and suspicion and she was constantly on the lookout for signs of moral decay or corruption in her offsprings' behaviour. Many a time Danny and his siblings would be watching a half decent film on TV and, no matter where their mum was in the house, if there was the slightest whiff of a sex scene, she would somehow magically, perhaps even tragically, appear and, with all the self-righteousness of an avenging angel, declare, 'This is filth. Turn it off immediately,' and that was that. Her response to 'Top of the Pops' was severe enough but any mention of Benny Hill and she almost foamed at the mouth. Danny felt quite sorry for his dad because he knew that he had quite enjoyed the slapstick humour and sexual innuendo of Benny – that and the Carry On films – but these little avenues of pleasure had been closed down when Danny's mum had cottoned on to the 'perverted' content of the programmes. The Venn diagram of TV shows that she approved of was fairly narrow. The Waltons, Little House on the Prairie and the occasional Agatha Christie whodunnit got through her censorship process but she was more of a reader – books set in the Regency period seemed good for the soul, Jane Austen and Georgette Heyer being thoroughly respectable literature.

She was an educated woman and a qualified nurse but she had given up her profession once the kids had come along, Mr O'Connell being the sole breadwinner now – a timekeeper for Glasgow City Corporation. Consequently, money was tight and Faifley their domicile. Mrs O'Connell had never fully accepted the housing scheme as home, her gaze often drifting beyond the horizon with a deep yearning to improve her family's lot, her ambitions for her kids to escape being the driving force behind her conviction that high standards, principled behaviour and the pursuit of academic excellence would be a passport to a better life for all the O'Connells. She had a vision for the future and she was uncompromising in her pursuit of it.

'No Adidas T-shirt. That's my final decision. Now, I'm sure you have some piano practice you need to do. Grade 8 piano is not going to walk up and shake you by the hand.'

'Well... mum... I said to Charlie that we'd go for a cycle ride this afternoon. It is Saturday, after all.'

'His name is Charles, Daniel, not Charlie. Just as your name is Daniel, not Danny. I'm sure his mother and father call him by the name with which he was christened.'

Danny had been in the company of Charlie's family on various occasions and he had heard them calling him various things – Charlie, Chick, Chuck, Chuckles, Chancer and a few other choice soubriquets – but he had never heard them call him Charles.

'Well, I suppose it is Saturday afternoon, so some exercise

would do you good. Is Charles coming up to Faifley or are you going down to Duntocher... yet again.'

The 'yet again' seemed somewhat barbed, a pointed comment that articulated a deep apprehension that Danny, in rubbing shoulders with the gallus Charlie, was sliding on a slippery slope towards plebian mediocrity. She did recognise the irony of someone living in Faifley looking down their noses at those in Duntocher but that did not stop her doing it anyway.

'We're actually going to meet up at the Cochno Road and have a wee cycle round the Edinbarnet Estate.'

'Very good. And since your friend is in this neck of the woods, perhaps he would like to come for lunch after your cycle ride. I think it's high time I met this Charles Harkness...'

<hr />

'WHAT THE HELL, DANNY? YOU'VE GOT TAE BE KIDDIN' ME. MEET yer maw! I'd rather be slapped on the face wi' a wet fish. Why does she want tae meet me, anyways?'

The two boys were cycling side by side along the wide track that circumvented the grand country mansion that was Edinbarnet house, part of an estate that had been bought by Glasgow University for its Vet College and sat on a hill high above Faifley. It was a bright autumnal morning but a dark cloud had just scudded across the mind of Charles Harkness.

'It's *anyway*, Charlie, not *anyways*. You can't get away with using slang.'

'Slang? Slang? This is the way I talk. And, by the way, so do you, China. Don't start wi' aw that snobby shite.'

'And you can't say *shite*. At least, not in front of her. She wouldn't like it.'

'Aw forgive me for breathin', big man. I'll mibbe just say *jobby* instead o' shite.'

'That wouldn't make sense – *aw that snobby jobby*. Just doesn't sound right, does it. *Shite* is a much better word when you think about it. It's so much more versatile.'

'Whit ye jibeerin' aboot, ya big toley? Naw, I'm no daen it. I'm pure keechin' myself. Everybody knows your maw is...'

Charley tried to find the right word or expression, one that would not cause too much offense yet would capture her intimidating demeanour.

'My maw is what?'

'... is a wee bit stuck-up. I mean, you're no' even talkin' right today. You've gone all la-di-da and pronouncin' everythin' right.'

Danny had to concede this. 'Aye, I knaw... Sorry. Yes, I know - but if I don't practise talking properly while I'm in your company then I'll end up slipping up in front of her and that might not end well for me. Listen, if you don't do this, she might very well stop me being friends with you – she's that much of a hard liner. So, you might as well just bite the bullet and try and be on your best behaviour – whatever that might be.'

'Geez, Danny. I've got a bad feelin' aboot this. Whit if she doesnae take tae me? I mean, is it like royalty in the old days and she just chops off yer heid?'

Danny had never really seen Charlie like this before. Normally he could look anyone in the eye and hold his own but the prospect of coming face to face with Mrs O'Connell was evidently terrifying him.

'Well, look at it from my point of view. It's doubly terrifying for me. I'm going to be sitting there on a knife edge wondering what verbal diarrhoea's going to come out of your mouth while simultaneously cacking myself as to what line of enquiry my mum is going to pursue with you. However, let's look on the bright side. She's a good cook.'

'Aw, that's aw right, then. That's just the bees knees. At least when I throw up on her cos I'm so terrified, I'll know it tasted good. If I do this, Danny, you owe me one.'

'Well, it's one less you owe me after all that you've done of late.'

'Aye, ok. But just remember, Danny – I am who I am and I'm no ashamed o' it.'

'*Not ashamed of it*, thank you very much. And by the way, it's Daniel and not Danny.'

'Aw aye, an' whit rhymes wi' Danny? Cos that's whit you are, ya big fud.'

⌁

DANNY'S MUM STOOD BY THE BACK DOOR OF O'CONNELL'S terraced house in Auchnacraig Road. Her son was cycling up the hill towards the back gate, a small dark-haired boy cycling beside him. First impressions were not good. Firstly, the dark hair was well below collar length, a faint whiff of the hippy culture irritating her nostrils; secondly, he was riding a Chopper bike, a ridiculous looking contraption that was all 70s style and little substance, her own son riding a thoroughly reliable and safe Raleigh Tourer – dull looking but perfectly functional; and thirdly, the boy was wearing an Adidas T-shirt, yellow with blue stripes, the sort of popular apparel that assaulted her eyes at every street corner in Glasgow, Clydebank and Faifley. It was like a uniform for yobbos. Still, for Daniel's sake, she should give him the benefit of the doubt. Charles was a product of his environment, after all.

'Good afternoon, Charles. Lovely to meet you,' she said as the boys pushed their bikes into the back garden. 'I've heard so much about you from Daniel.'

She held out her hand and Charlie stared at it momentarily, wondering if he should kiss it, bow to it or even curtsey in front of it, such was the regal authority of the lady before him.

'How do you do, Mrs O'Connell. The pleasure is all mine.'

Charlie had seen 'My Fair Lady' on the telly the week before and thought this is the way posh people talked, the strangulation of vowels in *How do you do* not a kick in the pants off Liza Doolittle's early attempts at a high-born accent. He decided the best bet was to shake her hand and await developments. Danny's mum smiled, 'Well, thank you, young man. Shall we go inside and have lunch?'

'I think that is a first class idea, Mrs O'Connell. Please lead the way.'

She turned and strode up the garden path to the back door. Danny was gawping at Charlie:

'Whit ye daen? That's OTT. Are ye extracting the Michael?'

'Naw, I'm just getting' in character – the character you want me tae play by the way.'

'Aye, but mibbe reel it in a bitty.'

'Christ, there's no pleasin' some people,' as he stepped into the lioness' den.

After fixing Charlie and Danny a drink of Lemon Creamola foam in the kitchen, Mrs O'Connell led them into the living room, in the corner of which a table had been set. Charlie's stomach lurched, not from the cloying sweetness of the fizzy drink, but the thought of having to endure a dinner table cross-examination.

'If you take a seat, I'll bring in the soupe a l'oignon in a minute.'

The two boys sat down, Charlie's eyes widening with terror when he saw the white linen cloth and an array of utensils on the surface, like a set of surgeon's tools laid out before an operation. In the Harkness abode, Charlie's family were not ones for sitting at tables, preferring to eat their 'scran' in front of the telly each night. Food was functional - mince and tatties, sausage beans and chips being examples of the staple diet – and it was consumed while digesting what the BBC or ITV dished up on the gogglebox. He had never seen such a formal arrangement of cutlery before. There seemed to be knives within knives, forks within forks, spoons below spoons, a dizzying selection of plates and dishes and baskets and bowls and salt and pepper cruets and a whole load of other things that he didn't know whether to shake or pat or stick or twist.

'Holy shit, Danny. This is Faifley, no' Buckingham Palace. Whit am I suppose tae dae here?'

'Just watch me and follow what I do.'

Mrs O' Connell appeared with two bowls of hot steaming brown liquid with wee bits of peeled onion in them. Charlie stared at it and then looked at Danny for guidance.

'You must wait until my mum sits at the table and then we can begin.'

She re-appeared with her own soup bowl and sat down.

'Daniel, would you like to say grace?'

Danny blushed, then bowed his head. Mrs O'Connell then bowed her head. Charlie thought it best to then bow his head, his eyes darting from side to side, trying to anticipate what was going to happen next in this surreal and somewhat bizarre ceremony.

'Bless us, oh Lord, and these thy gifts which we are about to receive, through Jesus Christ, Our Lord, Amen.'

'Amen.'

Mrs O'Connell glanced at Charlie who was staring morosely at the white linen cloth. She coughed. He looked up.

'Oh... aye right enough... Amen.'

'Right. After a hard cycle ride, I'm sure you boys are famished. Daniel, could you pass the bowl of croutons, please?'

Danny handed her the silver bowl of diced fried bread.

'Would you like some croutons, Charlie?'

'Oh yes, please, Mrs O'Connell. I just love cretins. My mother always says a meal isn't a meal without cretins.'

She just about managed to suppress a smile as Charlie used his fingers to lift the little morsels from the bowl. He was just about to shove them straight in his mouth when he thought better of it and watched Mrs O' Connell take one of her side spoons and scoop the croutons into her soup bowl.

'So, Daniel tells me you sit beside him in Maths. I'm well aware that this is not my son's best subject so I hope he's not holding you back.'

Charlie paused before he replied to this. He wondered if this was a trap. He glanced at Danny who, at that point, was helping himself to more 'cretins'.

'Eh, not at all, Mrs O'Connell. In fact, Danny..., I mean Daniel is a big help to me, especially when it comes to Geometry. Every Monday morning, we work well together and he always seems to have a head for shapes way beyond anything that I can manage. Is that not right, Daniel?'

'Oh yes, Charles. We are such a good team, are we not. Always bouncing mathematical ideas off each other.'

Mrs O'Connell knew fine well the two boys were trying desperately to say the right things and behave in the correct manner and, as she served the various courses at lunch, she found herself warming to the young lad sitting to her right. He was rough around the edges to be sure and didn't have a clue about table manners, but there was a deep-seated desire to get it right for his friend, a willingness to put himself through a labyrinth of etiquette and convention in order to cement a relationship that obviously meant a lot to both of them.

'And what ambitions do you have in life, young Charles?' she asked after they had finished a dessert of blanched pear in a raspberry coulee, possibly the most wonderful thing Charlie had ever tasted.

'I want to become a professional golfer but my mum and dad just want me to get an apprenticeship in John Brown's or with British Rail.'

'Well, no disrespect to your parents, Charles, but you hang on to your dream. Life puts obstacles in our way but if you can find a way to overcome them, you should grab it with both hands. Daniel says you are an exceptional golfer and if God has given you that talent, you should make use of it.'

'Thank you, Mrs O'Connell. That's very kind of you. And thanks for a lovely meal.'

As Charlie disappeared down the street on his Chopper bike, Mrs O'Connell and Danny waved cheerily at him, Danny relieved that the two friends had survived the matriarchal grilling, Mrs O'Connell happy that her son's taste in friends was sound. She looked at her boy and placed her hand on his shoulder.

'Daniel?'

He turned his head towards her.

'What colour of Adidas T-shirt did you say you wanted?'

8

THE REVENGE OF THE SARDINE

'P ass the ball, Danny... Get rid o'it... Gie it tae Buckley... Ah for Gawd, sake, ya big twat...'

The weekly torment that was S3 PE had come round again and Danny, as usual, was letting the side down. It wasn't that he was averse to kicking a football – he quite liked running about, toe poking and scuffing the ball whenever it happened to bounce in his direction. What he hated was the screaming and shouting aimed at him and, seemingly, him alone if he had possession of the ball. His belief in the brotherhood of men was severely shaken every time he ran out from the changing rooms of the PE block. Humanity's finer instincts were then left at the touchline and democracy took to the hills.

Danny didn't see why he should not have as equal a share of time kicking the Mitre about as anyone else on the pitch but it would appear that no one else shared this egalitarian view of the beautiful game. The cry of 'Gie it tae Buckley' was the refrain that rang out across the windswept pitch week in, week out and he steadfastly refused to 'Gie it tae Buckley'. Not that he had anything against Master Buckley per se – in fact he recognised that this lad had talent – it's just that once he got a hold of the ball, no one else was able to touch it. Buckley could dribble and caress the ball with the finesse of a Pele or a Socrates, feinting one way then the other, his balance and poise 'sheer poetry in motion' as the PE staff would regularly cry. But O'Connell had a problem with this – he firmly believed the game was a team game and he was going to stick to that principle. He was part of the team and he would have his moment of participation, no matter what, even if it meant being subjected to verbal broadsides. Danny was also well aware that every time the ball came anywhere near him, its general progress towards the opposition goal was short-lived. If Buckley had a prodigious talent in holding onto the ball, O'Connell had an equally impressive skill in giving it away.

So, it was with a bit of relief that he suddenly realised that he needed the toilet, his mother having rather foolishly given him an extra slice of sardines on toast that morning. The customary sardines on toast on a Thursday morning was, without question, a tasty treat but, as with all of life's little pleasures, there was always a price to pay, namely the commotion at the back of the Maths class, period 1, when Charlie and the back three rows of the class would bemoan the 'silent but violent' leaking of gas from O'Connell's sphincter. His friend's eyes would water as he covered his nose with his arm and rushed to the front of the room to escape the noxious fumes with the pretext that he had to sharpen his pencil. O'Connell was fortunate that Gleeson had lost his sense of smell in a rock-climbing accident in his 30's, when he fell off the Whangie in the Kilpatrick Hills while trying to impress a young lady. If the Maths dominie had retained the power of his snifter then Danny would have been belted from here to kingdom come such was the poisonous nature of the farts, so lethal, conjectured Charlie, that WW1 would, indeed, have been over by Christmas if Danny's backside had been used as chemical warfare by the allies.

So, with a bit of a scuttling motion to his jog back to the PE block, Danny reached the safe harbour of the second cubicle on the left, just in time before the storm broke – and what a tempest it was. The bottom dropped out of Danny's world with a resounding 'Splamooosh', followed by a residual squirting that even O'Connell found somewhat alarming such was its liquid intensity. 'Must have been a bad sardine in there, mum,' thought the young lad to himself. The reek of contaminated oily fish that had passed through the hyperactive intestines of a teenager who had just been running around a football field for the last half an hour filled the changing rooms with an almost tangible smog of putrefaction. 'Woooof,' said Danny out loud in recognition of his ability to turn his rear end into a weapon of mass destruction. He turned and looked down at the scene of devastation he had created in the toilet bowl. 'Better flush that away quick before the others get back,' he murmured to himself and quickly yanked the chain. Unfortunately, he yanked it so hard, the chain and the handle came away from the cistern above his head. 'Shit!' he cried out, the profanity never having been used in the history of profanities in such a fitting context.

He heard voices in the distance, the tell-tale signs that the game was over and the boys were returning to the PE block. 'Oh, bugger,' he mumbled. He grabbed a few sheets of Izal toilet paper and proceeded to wipe his backside. Now, to the uninitiated, perhaps a few words of explanation are needed to explain what the delights of Izal toilet paper were. Izal Medicated Toilet Tissue was the preferred method of cleaning bottoms in all comprehensive schools across Scotland. They had the texture of hard tracing paper and aside from the fact that they had almost no absorbency, after wiping one's derriere with a few sheets of these, one would have difficulty in sitting down for a week. Long before the expression 'Ripping someone a new one' was used, Izal tissue had cornered the market in it. Danny quickly swiped his arse a few times, wincing heroically with each upward stroke. He threw the grey and brown tissues into the bowl, covering up the dirty protest that he had made seconds earlier. He hoisted up his Y-fronts and his football shorts, hopped out of the cubicle and ran to the fourth cubicle, jumped into it and locked the door. He reckoned that if he created some distance between himself and the scene of the crime, then no one would suspect it was him.

The rest of the class had now entered the changing room and, sure enough, the reaction was instantaneous.

'Aw, Jesus Christ, whit the hell is that… Aww that's mingin' so it is… Somehin's died in here… Whoever did that should get a boot in the baws.'

Danny decided that he would press home the advantage and flushed the chain – successfully for the first time that day. He unlocked the door and stepped out to be met with about twenty angry faces glowering at him.

'Wis that you that did that in there, O'Connell, ya manky big bas…'

'It wisnae me lads, honestly. It wis like that when I got here. I reckon it wis one o' they wee first years that are oot there doin' cross country running. They cannae control their bowels.'

Many still looked sceptical but blaming first years was always a legitimate excuse for most things that went wrong in the school so the PE boys decided to let it slide.

'Aye, I bet it wis that wee speccy wan that speaks with the posh voice. Wait 'til I get a haud o' the wee shitemaster.'

Danny breathed a sigh of relief, went over to his bag and started to get changed. This particular time slot in the PE lesson was known by all the lads as The Danger Zone. It never failed to amaze O'Connell that in any other subject, the school was run like a Stalag camp, the constant sense that one was being watched by the guards and that a spotlight would be shone immediately on any deviation from acceptable behaviour. However, in PE, the teachers thought it perfectly acceptable to head into their little teaching base just off the changing rooms where they would promptly shut the door and leave the boys to their own devices. There must have been a Manual for Teaching that had been written in Victorian times that stated that after vigorous physical activity, it would be character building for young men to be left alone, crammed in an enclosed space, where they would strip off and then take part in a Survival of the Fittest competition where the bullies and thugs were the rule makers and bone breakers.

Danny was part of this class for just one period in the week but what was particularly challenging was the fact that the lads he shared the lesson with were known as The ROSLA boys. ROSLA stood for the Raising of the School Leaving Age, a desperate government initiative to keep the unemployment figures down by raising the age of departure from full time education from 15 to 16. All of these boys were non-academic – their only interest was to leave and get an apprenticeship in the local shipyards or start their training as tradesmen. A small percentage would inevitably end up in Barlinnie. They were like caged beasts. Danny had ended up in the same class because he was the only pupil in S3, male or female, who had decided to take Music as a subject and, consequently, his timetable was skewed in such a way that the only PE class was with these guys. In the cauldron of testosterone that was the changing rooms, the level of physical and verbal abuse would bubble and froth and sometimes spill over. Two Neanderthals ruled the roost – Hutton and Haggart – and if you caught their eye in the wrong way, expect backlash. Whipping the backsides of the weak and vulnerable with a wet towel was the default form of tribulation but sometimes Hutton and Haggart liked to get up close and personal, twisting nipples so hard that they would bruise for weeks. A swift unexpected punch in the testicles was another favourite and, as the victim doubled up in pain, the dynamic duo would follow it up with the dreaded mantra 'One for flinching' which would inevitably be accompanied by a slap on the side of the head. The level of cruelty was worthy of The Old Testament, Hutton and Haggart being Clydebank's very own Gods of Wrath and Retribution.

Danny was both surprised and relieved that he was always spared any rough treatment. Even though he would never win any prizes for sporting excellence, the ROSLA boys seemed, bizarrely, to have collectively made Danny exempt from any rough stuff. They were the ones that had given him his nickname Mozart. They had witnessed him playing the piano at assembly a few times now and, somehow, counter-intuitively, they gave him a free pass, perhaps recognising a talent that rose above the quotidian drudgery of their own lives. They seemed to be quite content on inflicting pain and suffering on their own type, allowing Danny to get on with whatever it was he did the rest of the week.

However, today, after the Revenge of the Sardines incident, Danny thought it prudent to change as quickly as possible and get out of Dodge. He wheeched off his football top, shorts and Y-fronts and quickly shoved them in his school bag, rummaged around its innards and pulled out a clean pair of underpants. His mother, God bless her, was always obsessed with providing her offspring with clean underwear, especially, for some odd reason, in the event of a road accident and being taken to hospital. Danny could never understand why doctors would be obsessed with whether a patient had a spare pair of clean Y-fronts, especially if they were lying on the operating table with their leg smashed to smithereens.

Although the PE staff always instructed the boys to shower, no one ever did. The S3 male cohort all bought into the theory that showers were for Nancy boys but, deep down, most simply didn't want to shower because a) the water was always Baltic b) the pink crusty carbolic soap stank to high heaven and c) no one really wanted to compare their length and girth in case of inadequacy. He quickly got dressed and, as far as he was concerned, just in time. Hutton and Haggart were swaggering their way towards him.

'Aw right, Mozart? How's it hangin'?'

Danny was not sure how to answer this, fearful that whatever it was that was hangin' was about to be given a swift and painful boot.

'Fine, lads, fine.'

'Aye, well, it's no' you we're after so don't keech yer pants.'

'If only you knew,' Danny thought to himself.

'It's this wee jobby that we want tae talk to.'

Standing behind Danny was the diminutive figure of Gary Pullar, an inoffensive and happy-go-lucky wee chap who was not, obviously, blessed with brains but had a sunny disposition that would serve him well in life. Today, however, was not going to go well for Gary, for something, it would appear, had deeply offended the sensibilities of Hutton and Haggart.

'We've heard somethin' that's upset us, Pullar. Whit team dae ye support?'

If there was one question in the West of Scotland that could make your blood turn to ice it was this one. If you were in the right company, it would be a cause for bonding and comradeship; in the wrong company, your life could be on the line. What made the question a curious one in this context was that everyone at school just assumed your colours were green and white, and not royal blue. It was a binary choice and, if you went to a Catholic school, it was bloody obvious who you supported. Hutton and Haggart were obviously working on some information that had been leaked to them.

Pullar stared at the two knuckledraggers.

'Whit is it tae you two?'

Haggart smacked him on the side of the head.

'Answer the question, ya wee prick, and don't get smart.'

'Well, if you really must know, I'm a Partick Thistle supporter and proud of it.'

Pullar was indeed a Jags man and had been since his dad had taken him to Firhill when he was six. The confession was greeted with stunned silence. The two H's simultaneously shook their heads. Hutton stepped menacingly towards him.

'Aye that's whit we heard.'

He leaned in close to Gary, so close he could smell his rancid breath:

'Whit are you anyway… a poof?'

Only in the West of Scotland could 'coming out' as a Partick Thistle supporter be equated with homosexuality.

Danny scurried out of the changing rooms just as Hutton had pinned Pullar against the wall and Haggart was bending the young boy's right forefinger backwards at an angle that predicated dislocation. A visceral scream followed O'Connell down the dark corridor and out into the playground. He gulped in the fresh air, leaving behind the foetid atmosphere and suppressing a desire to throw up.

He realised he was already late for the next class so he scurried across the playground in the direction of The Modern Languages department. Thursday, period 4, was always in The Language Lab, a recently installed state of the art classroom divided into 30 narrow booths within which each pupil was cocooned in their own little learning space. Once comfortably ensconced, they had to place headphones over their ears and converse with some recorded disembodied voice, intoning into their individual microphones, 'Jean-Pierre, mon frere, est dans la cuisine.' or 'Foufo, le chien, est dans le jardin.' Danny often thought that the French had the most pathetic names for their dogs – no one roundabout where he lived called their dog Foufou – more like, Rex, Butch, Lassie or Bruno – proper doggy names with a bit of bite to them, not something as effete and limp-wristed as Foufou. Anyway, all the kids enjoyed the

Language Lab, it wasn't teacher-led, you could go at your own pace, and it had the added attraction of feeling hi-tech.

O'Connell rushed into the classroom, apologised to Brundell, the French teacher, and shuffled to the row of booths at the back of the classroom. Charlie was already sitting in his space, establishing that Marie-Claire was 'dans la chambre.' Danny was mildly curious as to what Marie-Claire was doing in la chambre but thought he'd better not distract Harkness since distraction was the subject that his friend needed no practice in. He placed his bag at his feet, in between his booth and Charlie's, then took out his jotter from his bag. Wrapping his ears in the padded embrace of the headphones, he attempted to catch up with the rest of the class, glad that some sort of order had been re-established after the mayhem of the previous period.

Brundell walked around the room, happy that there was a buzz of meaningful activity, each child gamefully employed. This was his favourite lesson of the week – minimal input from him; maximum effort on the part of the kids. He was one of the teachers the kids regarded as cool because he never used the belt, preferring to use satire and caustic humour to keep order. Some thought he was a tad arrogant on account of his 'strut'. He had a ram-rod straight back and seemed to almost swagger when he walked around the classroom. This was not because of any military bent – the simple fact of the matter was that he'd fallen from the first floor of a hotel balcony in the Costa Brava during a drunken party a couple of years previously and broken his back. This particular morning, he walked his walk to the back of the classroom where O'Connell and Harkness (two characters you always had to keep an eye on, he mused to himself) sat concentrating on speaking and listening to French, for once behaving themselves. Brundell thought to himself, 'God's in his heaven and all's right with the world.' However, if there is one thing a teacher should never do, is count their proverbial chickens.

As he turned to make his way to the front of the class, something caught his eye. Poking out from O'Connell's school bag was an *objet* so grotesque he felt compelled to take a closer look. Danny was yabbling away into the microphone and was completely unaware that his teacher was bending over and peering, like some latter day Hercule Poirot, at a pair of Y-fronts with the most offensive skid marks he had ever seen. They had, obviously, been white at one stage in the not too distant past but there now seemed to be more smudged skid than clean cotton on show and what was even more revolting was the realisation that with the strip light above his head reflecting off its glistening moist surface, the brown marks were undoubtedly fresh. He tapped Danny on the shoulder.

'O'Connell. What the hell are those?'

Brundell pointed at the offending Marks and Spencers' pants and Danny looked down at his magnum opus.

'Oh cripes… sorry, sir,' muttered Danny as he reached down to gingerly poke the Y-fronts back in his bag.

But he was too late.

Charlie, with nimble fingers that a pick-pocket would have been proud of, lifted up the stinky drawers between thumb and forefinger and launched them into the air.

In the days, months and years to follow, Danny would re-live this moment in his nightmares, and every time he remembered it, the whole episode would re-play in extra slow motion, the whole sorry incident permanently imprinted in his mind.

The Y-fronts pinged back and forth across the classroom. It landed on shoulders, it landed on desk tops, it landed on the formica panels that divided the booths – but no matter where it landed, it was greeted with shrieks and squeals and screams and squawks, both of the male and female variety. Brundell and O'Connell watched, teacher and pupil both helpless in the face of the bedlam that was now unfolding, mouths agape, held transfixed in the moment, a moment of sublime chaos and pandemonium.

Charlie sat back and watched his handiwork – no, it was more than handiwork - it was a masterpiece of anarchy, and a beatific smile radiated from his face.

This was his best wheeze yet.

Yet better was to come.

Just as the crumpled pants looked as if they were heading back towards Danny's corner of the room, like one of those dormant reptiles snatching a bug in a nature film, wee McFadden's hand reached up and intercepted them in mid-flight. He twirled them around his head like helicopter blades then hurled them towards the front of the class.

It is hard to imagine that anyone could have managed to remain on task within the Language Lab that morning, but there was one girl, and one girl only, who had been oblivious to all the commotion playing out behind her.

And this girl was Catherine Mathieson, the girl who Danny had never conquered yet still secretly coveted.

Catherine was listening, through her headphones, to the fascinating revelation that 'Foufou aime des os,' when she felt something soft flumping onto the top of her head. The whole class froze in sweet anticipation as they watched the back of Catherine's head move to the left, then to the right, then upwards towards the ceiling, evidently seeking the source of her confusion. She lifted her right hand and placed it on her crown, patted it a couple of times, then plucked whatever it was that had alighted on her pate. She stared at it momentarily trying to compute what exactly it was she was holding in her hand.

And then realisation dawned.

It was a primeval scream, Hitchcockian in intensity, the indelible image of deep-seated brown skid marks instantly scarring the young girl's mental fortitude. She dropped them, ripped off her headphones, then rushed out the door, whimpering like a French poodle.

Two boys sat side by side at the back of the class, one doubled-up with laughter and unalloyed happiness, the other, once again, with mortification and embarrassment. Mr Brundell stood beside O'Connell clutching his pair of stinky Y-fronts. He looked impassively into the middle distance as he handed them to Danny, muttering, 'For God's sake put these away, O'Connell... and we'll say no more about it.'

As Danny shoved his soiled pants into his bag, it dawned on him that now and forever more, there would be two things, truly and indubitably, consigned to the dustbin of history - Catherine Mathieson and sardines on toast.

9

SAUSAGES

'Now, Danny, there's nothing to be afraid of. You just have to relax, breathe in and let yourself go. Remember, we're here and we're looking after you.'

O'Connell peered over the side of the rock face and could see about twenty faces looking up at him. He didn't fancy this one bit, not one tiny bit.

A random selection of S3 boys had been given the opportunity to travel to The Garelochhead Outdoor Centre for a week-long outward-bound course. The randomness of the selection by the PE staff was highly questionable when one thought of the thugs and ruffians that could have ended up on the course. Such hoodlums being introduced to the finer points of canoeing, orienteering, hill walking and archery hardly bore thinking about. The group of boys who were 'lucky' enough to have their names drawn out of an imaginary hat by an imaginary hand were, generally speaking, decent enough kids. Although the teachers knew that Charlie and Danny could say and do daft things at inopportune moments, they fell into the 'likeable rogue' category and, consequently, were put down on the list of fortunate kids that were being given five days out of mainstream school to run about the hills above Garelochhead and swim by the shores of Loch Gare. Despite the eyesore that was the Faslane naval base a few miles south of the town and the knowledge that if WW3 broke out, the whole of that corner of Argyll and Bute would have been vapourised in seconds by the Russians, it was a bonny part of the world with expansive water, towering mountains and big horizons – quite simply, it felt a million miles away from Duntocher and Faifley.

The only blot on the landscape was the fact that Tommy Lang had somehow made it onto the minibus that Monday morning, the minibus that subsequently drove them from Clydebank, down the A82, through Dumbarton and Helensburgh to the residential centre. Charlie and Danny reckoned his dad was a friend of the head of PE, both members of the Knights of St Columba, the Catholic equivalent of the Masons. Whatever jiggery-pokery had happened behind the scenes, the reality was that Lang was there for the week, though his oppressive presence was slightly mitigated by the fact that his loyal henchmen were not with him – for once, he was flying solo. This did not stop him slagging off and denigrating everyone and anyone at any opportune moment.

'Bloody hell, O'Connell, ya big muppet. I reckon Puggy Shuggy could do a better job wi' wan arm than you,' he bellowed the first day as Danny's arrow either nose-dived into the ground or careered off at right angles as he tried to hit the target in archery practice. Danny being slim of build, did not have any upper body strength to pull the taught string back far enough, hence the skew-whiff squirty nature of his sorry attempts. To make matters worse, Lang, being the big bruiser that he was, hit the golden bull's eye with monotonous regularity.

The snide comments had come thick and fast the whole week – when Danny had stripped off to his swimming trunks to do the 50m challenge in the cold inkiness of the loch, Lang quipped, 'I've seen mair meat on a sparra's kneecap, ya big lanky beanpole. I 'hink we'll call you Biafran-boy.' African famine victims were not worthy of sympathy in Lang's perception of the world, only a source for barbed metaphor.

What made matters worse, though, was the fact that Lang was physically mature and seemed obsessed with his own body. He had started shaving when he was in S1 and, like a hog, had bristly hairs starting to appear on his back. By the middle of S2, his chest, if not quite shag pile, was, certainly, impressively hirsute. This was, of course, a source of great pride and braggadocio on his part. 'This is what a real man looks like', he would crow as he bent into a Charles Atlas pose, bulging his biceps and flexing his pectorals. Although the rest of the boys knew nothing of homo-eroticism at the time, Lang's narcissism felt odd, peculiar, queer to the rest of the lads. They just couldn't quite put their finger on it.

Because he was physically strong, he excelled at many of the activities during the day, but he was truly in his element in the evenings when the boys were eventually packed off to their dormitories. There were fifteen bunk beds in their dormitory and Lang would strut up and down the wooden floor in just his Jockey shorts, going into other boys' bags and pinching their Twixes and Mars Bars. The first night, he was in his element - while O'Connell was in the shower room brushing his teeth, he rummaged in Danny's rucksack and extracted a pink water bottle that he held aloft with aplomb in front of the rest of the lads.

'Aww, look what Danny's mammy has packed for him. A nice wee hot water bottle. And pink – pink tae make the boys wink. Poor wee Danny – he might get cold tootsies, eh. Well, let's see what we can do, eh.'

He proceeded to unscrew the top of the bottle, gleefully urinated into it, screwed the top back on and placed it in O'Connell's sleeping bag, just as Danny finished his ablutions. If the hot water bottle had filled Lang's cup of mirth to the brim, what emerged from the shower room resulted in his joy overflowing. O'Connell was wearing a dark grey dressing gown, under which was a pair of navy-blue polyester pyjamas with red trimmings, the whole ensemble finished off with sheepskin moccasin slippers. The pyjamas were buttoned right up to his neck and, as he emerged from the shower room, the whole dormitory turned to gowk at him. All the rest of the boys had had the nous to realise that in the crucible of forging an image for oneself in front of one's S3 peers, less was more. Most of the lads just wore their Y-fronts and a t-shirt. Danny's mother had told him in no uncertain terms that he had to wrap up warm, late October in The Highlands being a cold place.

'Look at the state o' this,' erupted Lang. 'Hey grandad, where's yer zimmer? Can I get ye yer pipe, ya geriatric fud? How aboot a cup o' Ovaltine? Whit a massive diddy you are, O'Connell. A total wanker, man.'

To be fair, even Charlie covered his hand over his eyes as the other boys hooted heartily, such was his embarrassment for this public display of his friend's naivety. He had taken the top bunk and, as Danny approached him, running the gauntlet of Lang's witticisms, Charlie murmured, 'Dump the hot water bottle, Danny. It's in yer sleeping bag. Dump it as soon as you can. Don't ask.'

So, it was very much like that during the week. Not one single pupil ever thought of talking to a teacher about Lang's relentless verbal blitzkrieg, the one simple rule in a schoolboy's code d'honneur being – you don't snitch. If you ever grassed on a fellow pupil, that was it – you would be ostracised forever more, sent to the Siberian wastelands of obscurity, never to be trusted again, branded a clipe for life.

All things considered, though, during the day, Danny enjoyed the fresh air and the outdoor activities despite Lang's sniping; and he had also learned one very important lesson from the evenings' experiences – mother does not always know best, especially when it comes to the idiosyncratic behaviour of adolescent boys. It was with a heavy heart and maybe a little pang of homesickness that he stuffed his jim-jams and dressing gown into his voluminous rucksack on the Tuesday morning, a subconscious admission that he was packing away part of his childhood, a further fraying of the umbilical cord, peer pressure trumping maternal love. He comforted himself by steadfastly and stubbornly wearing his moccasin slippers, a gesture of defiance against Lang's obsession with his standards of conformity.

Thursday being the penultimate day was also one of climax, the two most exciting and eagerly anticipated activities of the week being abseiling and the overnight camp-out. The talk the whole week was how terrifying the abseiling was going to be. Teenage boys' capacity for hyperbole and fabrication knew no bounds - the height of the rock they were to descend seemed to grow 40 feet each time it was discussed, so much so it had grown in their minds to be of Mont Blanc proportions. There were also stories of boys in other schools ending up as quadriplegics and paraplegics, wheelchair-bound victims of cack-handed instructors who had accidentally let go of the ropes too early. All of this was hogwash, of course, but it gained traction in the minds of the more gullible kids, Danny being one.

'Whit if they drop us from a great height, Charlie?' enquired O'Connell of his mate.

'Well, I reckon yer heid'll crack off the rocks and then yir body'll splat all over the place when you hit the grun, wi' bits o' brain and snot and shit everywhere.'

'Aw, naw, I'm no daen' this.'

'Will ye just listen tae yersel', Danny. These guys are experts. Nobody's gonnae get injured. It'll be fun, just jumping aff the side o' a cliff and bouncing down the rocks, like that guy in The

Milk Tray adverts – 'All because the lady loves Milk Tray.' Just think o' yersel' as James Bond. Anyway, ye'll never hear the end o' it frae Lang if ye cop out. That'd be worse than bein' in a wheelchair the rest o' yer life.'

With that ringing endorsement in his head, Danny reluctantly climbed aboard the minibus which was full of nervously nattering boys, expectancy and anxiety a heady cocktail which fuelled conversation.

'Who d'ye think'll chicken oot,' enquired Lang, 'I reckon it'll be O'Connell? I bet yer pure cackin' yersel', eh O'Connell?'

Lang proceeded to make clucking noises and flapped his arms like the wings of a chicken.

'Ignore him, Danny,' whispered Charlie, 'he's jus tryin' tae psyche ye out.'

'He's doin' a bloody good job o'it,' thought Danny.

Sometimes reality can outstrip the vast power of the imagination – but not often. The inner eye of the majority of the boys had pictured a cliff of El Capitan proportions. When they arrived at the crag, the sense of anti-climax was palpable. The rock face was about 20 metres high and from ground level did not seem to amount to much.

'Christ, I could jump off that and no' hurt mysel',' declared Lang, this itty-bitty bit of granite no match for his towering ego. There was almost a collective sigh of relief, with Danny's nervous, gurgling tummy settling itself somewhat.

However, it was only when the boys took the track that led round the back of the crag and then approached the ridge from the rear that the swagger and bombast somewhat dissipated. Once they looked over the edge, it was a different perspective and a different story.

'Cripes,' said Danny to Charlie. 'That looks an awfie way down.'

Charlie, who was a tad discombobulated himself, muttered, 'Ach, it's nothin'. Come oan, let's get kitted up.'

The lads put on their helmets and proceeded to listen attentively to the group leader as he explained the intricacies of the harness and the carabiners, belay devices and ropes, a new language, a vocabulary both exotic and stimulating, way more interesting and vital than *'Foufou est dans le jardin'*.

Over the next hour or so, one by one, the boys disappeared over the edge, the majority a little bit tentative in their first few steps, a few almost launching themselves with gay abandon, thrill seekers in their element. And as each one conquered their own fears and sated their own desire for adventure, the rag-tag bunch of disparate lads suddenly merged into a cohesive unit. Without any prompting from the outward-bound instructors, the boys egged each other on, shouting encouragement and reassurance.

'Come on, Charlie, you can dae it... That's it, Mikey boy, yer skooshin' this... Well done Big Pete, yer nearly there.'

For the adults, witnessing the transformation of sarcastic hard-hitting youngsters with a penchant for reductive humour to team players willing each other to succeed was both satisfying and heart-warming. They nodded approval and patted the kids on the back.

Towards the hour mark, only two figures were left at the top of the crag – Danny and Tommy. O'Connell had held back, watching and listening, anxiously trying to see what the best technique was for descent. Lang had gradually become quieter and quieter as the morning wore on, the mood of camaraderie and solidarity going against the grain of his philosophy of intimidation. As Danny turned his back on what seemed like an abyss, he placed the balls of his feet on the edge and cast a glance over his shoulder.

'Oh, shit, oh shit, shit, shit, shit.'

'It's all right sonny, we've got you. Just let yourself go.'

This was the crux of it and Danny knew it. To lean back into thin air and have one's life dangling at the end of a rope held by a stranger was an anathema to him. Trust didn't come easy to him, his school life being punctuated by countless betrayals and disappointments. Then, all of a sudden, he heard a voice from below, the distinct dulcet tones of Charlie, the source of so many of his humiliations. There was an almost manic intensity to Charlie's exhortations, a visceral pleading with him to lean back and step over the edge.

So, he did it.

Initially, it was just tiny baby steps, his buttocks so clenched he could have cracked walnuts with them, but once he leaned back and got the 60-degree angle against the rock face there was no stopping him. Towards the foot of the cliff, he even started to relax, bend his knees and spring off the crag, applause and hearty cheering with every bravado bounce. The boys surrounded him and clapped him on the back and ruffled his hair when he took off his helmet. His legs were a bit wambly but his chest was puffed out with pride.

'Well done, ya big dunkey's whalloper. That wis quality,' Charlie exclaimed, punching him playfully on the arm, comparing his friend to an asinine phallus about as affectionate a term of endearment as you could find. He climbed out of the harness, unclipped the belay devices and stood back, looking upwards to see the final descent.

Lang was all kitted up and stood peering over the edge. A cold gust of wind buffeted his face, a face with such a look of terror etched on it that the boys instantly fell silent. A querulous voice floated down in breeze.

'I cannae dae this… I cannae dae this.'

They had all heard it but they couldn't believe it.

The instructor looked into his eyes.

'Listen, Tommy. A big strong guy like you? This should be nothing. All you need to do is turn around and relax.'

'I telt ye I cannae dae it.'

The instructor placed his hands on Tommy's shoulders.

'Dinnae touch me, dinnae touch me.'

There was a high-pitched screeching intensity to Tommy's voice as it rang around the crags and the rocks.

'I cannae dae it,' he squealed one last time as he stepped away from the edge, tears streaming down his cheeks.

There were no shouts of encouragement, no cries of support. Just the sound of the wind whipping up the hillside and the lonely squawk of a seagull.

'Well... bugger me,' murmured Charlie but just loud enough for the other boys to hear. 'Who woulda guessed? Greetin' like a wee lassie. Tommy Lang – yir finished, mate. Totally Donald Ducked.'

The rest of the boys shuffled and glanced sideways at each other. Charlie smiled.

'Oh dear, whit a shame, never mind.'

The group laughed heartily, a shared release of pent-up antagonism towards the guy that had, at one time or another, persecuted all of them physically, verbally and mentally.

As they wandered back towards the minibus, Charlie turned to Danny and mused:

'I guess it's true what they say – the bigger they are the harder they fall. Though you're the exception to the rule, ya big fud.'

The rest of the afternoon was spent preparing for the camping trip, an excursion into the wilds of Glen Fruin forest. The boys collected their tents, gas stoves and mini frying pans from the kit store and their dinner provisions from the kitchen. They were all on a high after the abseiling buzz, all, of course, except one. Tommy Lang, having morphed into a saturnine, gloomy shadow, detached himself from the now tight-knit group and wandered the corridors of the centre on his own. There was no banter, no slagging, no bad-mouthing emanating from him. He had retreated into himself, every possible vulnerability tucked away, withdrawn from public view. To add to his discomfiture, the boy with whom he should have been sharing his tent, had left the centre after the abseiling on account of an ailing grandfather back in Clydebank. Tommy would now be on his own.

The minibus rattled and bounced along the rutted forestry track. The boys peered out from its windows, eager to see where they were going to camp. They emerged suddenly from the phalanx of pine trees that lined the track into a clearing from which they could apparently see half of Scotland. In a wide panoramic sweep, they held their breath as they scanned the loch below them, the sun glinting off its surface, Ben Lomond and the Arrochar Alps in the distance jutting into the expansive sky. For many of these lads, this was the first time they had truly experienced the sheer scale and beauty of a Scottish wilderness.

'Room wi' a view, eh,' quipped Danny as he tramped about the tussocky ground with Charlie looking for a flat bit of ground to pitch.

'How about here?' Charlie said, pointing to a relatively level patch of grass.

'There's some sheep shite on it. I'm no sleeping on sheep shite,' announced Danny.

'Just kick it tae the side.'

'Why dae I have to clear up the sheep shite?'

'Ok, ya big wuss. I'll clear it and you can unpack the tent. Honestly, yer so high maintenance.'

'The instructors never tell ye aboot things like sheep shite. That should be in the small print or some'hin. Ye can go blind frae that stuff.'

'That's dog shite, ya muppet, not sheep,' said Charlie as he flicked the offending black crumpled blobs to a safe distance.

'This looks ok, just here,' announced Danny with the air of a man that was trying to talk with authority but deep down was pretty clueless as to what was really going on. 'An' do we point it away from the prevailing wind or is it intae the prevailing wind. I cannae mind whit he said.'

'Just stick it side oan, it willnae matter, will it,' asserted Charlie, the walking embodiment of foresight and planning.

Since Danny and Charlie were both virgin campers, the whole experience of putting up a tent took somewhat longer than the 15 minutes the instructors had given as an average time for completing the task. About three quarters of an hour later, a rather shaky looking orange erection with the passing resemblance to a triangular prism wobbled and shook in the gentle breeze, the guy ropes hanging low and loose on the ground.

'That looks the biz, eh Danny boy. Home, sweet, home.'

Danny looked at it with a large dollop of scepticism.

'If you say so, Charlie, but it looks right rickety tae me.'

'Och, stop yer greetin' and let's make dinner. Everybody else has nearly finished theirs and the smell o' scran's drivin' me nuts. Right – whit's in the bag?'

'Four sausages and a tin o' baked beans.'

'Braw. Let's do this then.'

They unwrapped the sausages from their clingfilm and stared at them as if it was the first time they had ever seen raw sausages. To be fair on them, it was the first time they had actually been away from home on their own, left to fend for themselves, no mothers or fathers to cook for them.

'Whit are we supposed to dae wi' them?' asked Danny.

'Cook them, of course.'

'How?'

'Ye stick them in the wee frying pan and put it on the stove.'

'Aye, but should we no take them oot their wrappers first?'

'Whit d'ye mean?'

'Well they've aw got some sort o' skin on them. I'm sure ye have tae peel the skin aff before cooking them. Otherwise, they'd aw catch fire and blow up in yer face.'

'Aye. Come tae think o' it, ye might be right. That skin looks kinda plasticky. Wouldn't like tae eat that. Must be like peeling bananas. It's the bit inside ye want. Ok, you take your two and I'll take mine.'

The two culinary geniuses proceeded to pick and tear at the sausage skin, painstakingly plucking at the offensive membrane, trying to release the succulence within.

'My meat's gone all floppy Charlie. It doesnae look like a sausage any more. D'ye think this is right?'

'Aye, it'll be fine. Once ye cook it it'll go back tae being sausage shaped, wait an' see. My maw told me ye've got tae cook this type o' meat thoroughly. I dinnae want food poisonin', not oot here in the wilds.'

After what seemed an eternity, the boys finally had two ragged, sorry-looking strips of pink processed pork in their hands.

'Right let's fire up the gas stove,' announced Charlie.

They unpacked the little stove and, after various attempts at striking matches that had become damp because Danny had left them lying on the wet grass, the little blue gas flame sputtered into life. They popped the mangled meat into the frying pan, hunger gnawing at their insides like some visceral rodent.

'Haw, ho, here we go,' declared Charlie.

They stared at the pan. Something didn't look right.

'That doesnae look right,' deduced Danny. 'What's happenin' tae the meat?'

Charlie had no answer to this vexing question. All he knew was that, before his very eyes, his dinner was shrinking fast at a phenomenal rate, the promised reincarnation of the juicy sausage failing to materialise. With much sizzling and fizzling, all that was left in the pan were dismal little blackened clumps and splotches of charred mincemeat.

'I reckon we shouldnae have taken off the skin, eh, Charlie.'

'No kiddin', Sherlock,' Charlie replied, looking dismally at the meagre morsels in front of him.

Taking a spoon each, they scooped up what was left of the sausage experiment and shoved the tiny portions in their mouths. In one gulp, they were gone.

'Danny, I swear tae God. We're gonnae die o' starvation oot here. There'll be nothin' but oor skeletons by the morra mornin'.'

'We've still got the baked beans.'

'OK, that's a lifeline, I suppose.'

After footering about with the tin opener for what seemed like another eternity, Danny prized open the lid, poured the beans into the frying pan and placed it on the stove. Alas, the base of the stove was not quite on the level and the frying pan and all its contents toppled sideways onto the grassy turf, the beans and tomato sauce spreading across the ground like a mini lava flow.

'Naw, naw, naw… quick… grab a spoon.'

The now desperate duo bent over and tried to ladle the cold beans onto their plate. Danny reckoned he had salvaged a respectable portion of them but in the fading light he failed to notice that a blob of sheep shite had infiltrated its way onto his plate. He scooped up a spoonful, shoved it in his mouth and instantly gagged. Spitting the revolting gruel onto the ground, he bent over and peered at it.

'Sheep shite, Charlie. Sheep shite. I've just put sheep shite in ma gob. You were supposed tae clear it aw. I'm gonnae go blind. I'm gonnae wake up like Stevie Wonder. Bugger this camping crap. Bollocks tae the whole thing.'

After calming down the slightly hysterical O'Connell, Charlie suggested that they go scrounging food from some of the other lads. Moving from one tent to another they soon realised that the others had finished eating earlier, by some distance, and they were all looking forward to building the camp fire with the instructors.

'This is dire,' said Danny, 'We cannae go the night without food.'

As it happened, there was still one boy whom they had not asked, deliberately avoiding him for obvious reasons. Tommy Lang had, bizarrely, pitched in close proximity to Harkness and O'Connell's tent. They had clocked this in their peripheral vision earlier but had not given it much thought, seeing as they were so wrapped up in their attempts at basic survival.

'Are you gonnae ask?' enquired Danny.

'Why me? Do I have tae do everythin'?'

'There's only wan o' him. Maybe he's got extra scran.'

'OK. We'll do it taegether. I'm so hungry, I don't care who I scrounge from.'

They approached Lang, who was sitting just inside his tent, staring morosely at the ground.

'Hi, Tommy,' said Charlie with as much bonhomie as he could muster, 'Danny and I had a wee accident wi' oor stove and, tae cut a long story short, we're pure Hank Marvin and got nae food. We were just wonderin' if you've got any left-over sausages or beans or whatever.'

Tommy looked at them quizzically, then reached into his tent and retrieved a plate that had a thick, juicy looking, perfectly cooked brown sausage sitting invitingly on it. The two boys licked their lips.

'Look at that, Charlie,' remarked Danny, 'The skin's still oan it. Who would o' thought, eh?'

Lang proceeded to pick up his fork, then pressed it into the tender meat, a little bit of grease oozing out of the prong marks. He held it front of his face and stared at it for a few seconds. It took all of Charlie and Danny's self-will to restrain themselves from grabbing it and tearing it apart.

'I had three sausages and a whole tin o' beans aw tae mysel', lads. Pure stuffed I was.'

'Lucky old you, Tommy,' remarked Charlie, his eyes locked on to the most beautiful sausage in the universe.

'But I reckon I'm no' that stuffed that I couldnae squeeze wan more in.'

And with that he crammed the whole sausage into his mouth and chewed and chewed and chewed, smiling as he did so, his revolting gob opening and closing, sticking his tongue out to reveal half-masticated meat.

'Whit a toley,' grumbled Charlie as they went back to their tent. 'I guess it's true whit they say aboot leopards and spots. I almost felt a wee bit sorry for him this mornin' but that's it. Once a fud, always a fud.'

As it was, the instructors came to the boys' rescue. They had plenty of left-over food and filled the lads' bellies with much needed sustenance – but on one condition: that they 'did a turn' round the camp fire and tell a funny story or crack a joke or sing a song. It was not a task, ordinarily, that was obligatory but, the boys having made a pig's ear of their dinner, needed to learn that there were consequences to their actions.

Having built and lit a good going camp fire, the team leader brought out the biggest bag of marshmallows the boys had ever seen. Piercing them with sticks, they were all enthralled in the act of cooking them on the glowing embers. Toasting them until golden brown, they were in seventh heaven popping them into their mouth, the hot crusty coating complementing the cooler soft mallow within. Somehow the tang of the fresh air made them taste all the sweeter. Danny, of course, managed to drop about three of them into the fire before he mastered the technique but by the time they had finished, the boys leaned back, replete, their tummies full, a ruddiness of fulfilment on their cheeks as the red glow of the flames reflected off their young faces.

O'Connell was instructed to sing for his supper and, music being his forte and having no mean voice, he stood up and launched into a rendition of the 'Jeely Piece' song. When it came to the chorus, twenty odd voices lustily averred that 'Ye canne fling pieces oot a twenty storey flat, seven hunner hungry weans will testify tae that, If it's butter, cheese or jeely, of the breid or pan, The odds against it reaching earth are ninety-nine tae wan.' A loud cheer went up at the end of the performance and all eyes turned to Charlie. Never one from shying away from the limelight, he stood up and, like a junior Billy Connelly, regaled his audience with a personal anecdote.

'I've got a wee hamster an' I call it Hammy. Hammy the hamster – dead original, like. Now, I've had wee Hammy goin' on four years noo and, for a hamster, that's pretty good goin', considering it was me that wis put in charge o'it. The thing is, I reckon I keep my Hammy young at heart wi' a wee game I play wi' him called Flyin' Hamster. Now, ye know the record turntables we aw' have at home. Wee Hammy loves sitting on that and whit he really likes is when I switch it oan tae 17rpm and he goes slowly roon and roon cleanin' his wee cute face, watching the world go by. What he likes even more is when I put it up tae 33 – he starts walking against the spin like he's oan some kinda treadmill. They're lazy wee buggers, hamsters – ye've got tae watch they don't get too fat so I reckon this is a hamster's answer tae goin' tae the gym. But Hammy's no finished yet. He cannae wait for me tae press the 45 switch. It's like us goin' on The Waltzers at The Kelvin Hall. He sort o' shuffles an' waddles an' tumbles across tae the edge o' the turntable and digs his wee claws intae the rubber, peerin' oe'r the side – cos he know whit's comin' next.'

All eyes were on Charlie, mouths agape.

'I flick 78 and, whoosh, Hammy goes wheechin' aff the turntable intae the air. Me, my brother, may maw and my daw, we all shout' – Charlie raised his arms like a conductor at the start of a symphony and on the down stroke a chorus of voices all yelled into the night sky, 'Flying Hamster' – 'and oor Hammy flies through the air wi' his wee paws stretched oot like some wee hamster superhero, and lands on the carpet, tummlin' his wulkies like a toty gymnast. Some people might think this is cruelty tae animals but I know my wee Hammy loves it cos he scurries back across the flair tae the record table and looks up at it, askin' for mair.

And that's the story of the one and only Hammy the 'Flyin' Hamster.'

A rousing cheer went up followed by rapturous applause, the hackneyed phrase 'Happy Campers' never having felt so apt. Only one figure sat apart from it all. Sitting in the shadows, with envious eyes narrowing to little slits in his face, was Tommy Lang. Not once did he laugh; not once did he smile; not once did he clap his hands. He stood up at the end of Charlie's monologue and slunk off into the darkness, climbed into his tent and zipped up the flaps.

The instructors signalled that it was time for the boys' kip and, after the physical and emotional rigours of the day, they did not put up any kind of resistance. Charlie and Danny wriggled into their sleeping bags and lay down on the ground sheet.

'Aw, bugger me. There's a dirty great big stone underneath my arse, Charlie.'

'Nae luck, big man,' Charlie yawned. 'Apart frae the sausages' fiasco, that was a braw day, eh?'

'Aye, Charlie boy. Not bad at all.'

As a hush descended over the campsite, there was only one more thing Charlie felt he had to do.

He sat up, resting his elbows on the ground and, at the top of his voice, shouted, 'Night, John Boy.'

From somewhere nearby, a disembodied voice rang out, 'Night, Mary Ellen.'

'Night, Jim Bob.'

'Night, Erin.'

'Night, Ben.'

'Shut it, the lot of you. Get tae sleep.'

And as the boys drifted off, all that could be heard was the wind rustling the branches of the nearby pine trees – that, and the faintest whimpering and weeping from the tent next to Charlie and Danny, the one belonging to Tommy Lang.

10

CHRISTMAS DANCE

By a cruel twist of fate, Danny O'Connell had missed the school Christmas dances when he was in S1 and S2. By the final week of the winter term, his energy levels were always low and his susceptibility to any virus doing the rounds was pretty high. He had succumbed to a bad dose of flu in first year, followed by a nasty cold in second year so he found the crescendo of excitement that was building in the S3 cohort in the weeks prior to the 1976 dance somewhat baffling, not having any point of reference or prior experience.

Charlie, on the other hand, was the practised expert in all things dance related.

'It's the mistletoe, Danny. If you get yourself in front of the right burd at the right time wi' a bit o' mistletoe, ye'll get a winch.'

The 'winch' was now the all-consuming obsession of many of the boys - which lassies might be up for it, which lassies were high face-value and which lassies you could just about get away with as far as being winchable. It never really occurred to the vast majority of lads that this was a two-way street and that the girls could have their own hierarchy of desirables. The self-obsession of the teenage boys precluded any notion that girls might be anything other than willing, passive recipients of the lads' irresistible charms.

'Don't the teachers stop you from kissing?' Danny enquired, the week before the big event.

'Aye, well, some o' them are on the lookout – Gleeson for sure - but it's aye dark and crowded in the hall and if ye can get behind a pillar or one o' the stage curtains, yer quids in. Anyways, most o' the teachers on the last Friday before Christmas are half-cut anyway. They're no' that bothered.'

Danny felt that divulging this bit of information to his mother might not be a good idea so, when he asked her if he could go to the dance and she asked him about the details of the big event, her son kept the reply reasonably vague.

'It's on the last Friday afternoon and it's S1-S3. They lump all the juniors in together and the teachers obviously keep an eye on everything. I've missed it the last two years, mum, so can I go this year... please?'

'Mmmm, and what is the dress code? School uniform?'

'No, no, no, mum. Causal. I can wear my Adidas T-shirt. That'll be fine.'

'No son of mine will go to a dance wearing sports gear. Your father was always immaculately dressed when we went dancing in our day.'

Danny had great difficulty imagining his parents in their prime enjoying themselves but what was more disconcerting was the 'No son of mine...' statement. That generally was the precursor to his mother taking control of the fine detail.

'Well, as part of your Christmas present, I'm happy to take you into Black's and buy you some new clothes for the dance. There will be many decent young girls in their party frocks, looking very pretty and respectable, so I would hate to think you would look out of place in such company.'

Danny had the distinct impression that his mother was

imagining her son alighting from his carriage and striding into the school hall, an eligible latter-day Mr Darcy to some grateful Elizabeth Bennett.

'Thanks, mum,' declared Danny with as much enthusiasm as he could muster. He knew that her promise 'to buy you some new clothes' had small print attached to it. What she really meant was that she would choose the clothes and she would turn out her boy in what she deemed acceptable.

And so, the Saturday before the dance, Danny found himself in Black's, the men's outfitters, in Sauchiehall Street. This was not a shop that had a sister branch in Carnaby Street, for sure. Every time Danny entered through its arched doorway, there was an oppressive hush that was almost ecclesiastical in intensity, not helped by the 'priests' who shuffled across its wooden varnished floorboards, little hobgoblins dressed in black suits with measuring tapes draped around their necks. They were all about 164 and, although they treated Mrs O'Connell with a disquieting obsequiousness, they looked on young Daniel with barely concealed antipathy, the boy's youthfulness an insurmountable barrier to customer relations.

'What can we do for you today, Mrs O'Connell?' enquired a Gollumesque creature, head tilted, shoulders bent in a servile stoop. For some odd reason, everyone seemed to whisper to one another in conspiratorial tones. In lowered voice, Danny's mum leaned in close to Gollum, and confessed, 'My son is going to his first school dance and I am looking for something suitable, something tasteful.'

'Certainly, Mrs O'Connell, delighted to be of assistance.'

Two judgemental eyes glowered at him, looking him up and down.

'This way, boy,' muttered Mr Charming and he led him to a little changing cubicle, pulled back the curtain and shoved him inside. After what seemed like half an hour, the curtain twitched and a hand clutching a pair of black trousers and a brownish looking top was thrust towards Danny.

'Try these on,' hissed the voice on the other side of the curtain.

Danny did as he was told and looked in the mirror. The top was a fawn-coloured woollen polo-neck, its high neck doubled over just under Danny's chin, its texture not unlike hessian, scratchy and prickly. Against his bare skin, its itchiness was almost unbearable. The trousers were heavy duty black corduroys, not quite drainpipe but not far off it. Danny reckoned that every single boy in the school would be wearing flares and an open neck Simon shirt or T-shirt. What Danny saw in the mirror was the antithesis of cool, the embodiment of dweeby dorkishness. He hated it.

'Oh, that is perfect,' exclaimed his mother when he slid out from behind the curtain. 'You look so smart, Daniel.'

'Yes, I do have an eye for this sort of thing,' squeaked Gollum.

'It's awful itchy,' revealed her son, a look of martyrdom on his face.

'Oh, if you put a vest on underneath it, you'll be fine.'

'But I'm really hot wearing it already.'

'That's just the shop lights. Anyway, it's winter. You need to wrap up. You don't want to catch a cold again, do you?'

And so, it was a done deal. The problem was Danny didn't feel he could complain that much. He knew that money was tight and that this was a stretch for his mum – indeed she had to put it on her account - a common way for parents to pay for their kids' clothes by paying it off in instalments over six months.

'I hope you know what a lucky boy you are,' were the parting words of the goblin outfitter as Danny trudged out of the front door. All of a sudden, the excitement of his first school dance had waned a little.

'Whit are you wearing, Charlie?,' enquired Danny on the Monday morning.

'Bay City Rollers high waistband flares with the wee tartan trimmings, black Simon shirt and platforms.'

'Oh,' murmured, Danny. 'I thought you said ye didnae like The Bay City Rollers.'

'Aye, well it's the music that's pish. Their breeks are pretty cool and the lassies, remember, love them. Whit aboot you?'

Danny hesitated, processing what the lassies might think of his mother's chosen style, her Kryptonite to the all-powerful Bay City fashion. 'Ah, well, ye'll have tae wait and see. I'll be fighting them aff, so I will.'

Danny's apprehensions concerning his attire on the big day faded somewhat over the next few days as his acne predicament worsened. He was starting to wonder if outbreaks of plookiness were related to stress. His face looked as if it had been pebble-dashed with red gravel by the Thursday night and he was wondering if he should bother going to the wretched dance. It just so happened that his sister, no stranger to this particular affliction, had bought a sun face lamp the week before, in the hope and belief that the UV rays would blitz the spots. Although the jury was out on this, Danny had reached Desperateville and decided that this was worth a gamble – what had he to lose, after all. Although his sister warned him that he should only spend a maximum of 30 seconds on his first sitting, Danny was not one for half measures. He pulled the little dark brown goggles over his eyes, plonked himself in front of the orange square, switched it on and sat for five minutes in front of its dazzling glow. He imagined himself waking up the following morning, plukes evaporated, his face tanned and flawless, like a bronzed Burt Reynolds without the moustache.

The reality was somewhat different.

When he awoke, giddy as an eight-year old on Christmas Day, he rushed into the bathroom and looked in the mirror.

What stared back at him was of Hammer House of Horror proportions. His face was on fire, burning hot, a blazing beacon of burgundy, his plukes agonizingly painful, each blackhead screaming against the violent surface heat of his cheeks. But the final masterstroke of degradation was the white rings around his eyes, pale circles left by the oval-shaped goggles, a racoon caught in headlights.

'That's it, mum. I'm not going,' he announced at breakfast. 'I can't face the world looking like this.'

'Now, Daniel, you're overreacting. Once you put on your nice new clothes, you'll be fine.'

After much debating of the matter, it was agreed that Danny could take the morning off and go to the dance in the afternoon, in the hope that the nuclear fission that was his face would be less radioactive by then. After a few hours of nervous scowling at himself in the mirror, the glow had diminished slightly but not enough for Danny to venture forth to win the heart of fair maiden.

'I can't do this mum, I just can't.'

Mrs O'Connell was not ready to give up on the day, after all, she had invested some capital in its hero.

'OK, I wouldn't do this ordinarily but since it's a bit of an emergency, we can try it out. I'll put a bit of make-up on you, quieten it all down. A wee bit of foundation should do the trick.'

With much grumbling and peevish bellyaching, Danny gave in to his mother's exhortations and she applied the cosmetics required.

'There – you look fine. No one will ever notice.'

Danny, by now past the point of actually caring, refused to look in the mirror for fear of cardiac arrest, and decided to get his dance gear on and literally face the music. He slipped on the white vest and pulled the polo neck jumper over his head. He could already feel the first prickles of heat against his skin. He then wriggled into the black corduroys and noticed that his mum had ironed a seam into the trouser legs. He shook his head but was now philosophically accepting his fate: 'Que sera, sera,' he muttered to himself.

'Have a lovely time,' his mum called as he trudged sullenly towards the bus stop to catch the No 48 to Ignominy.

The Christmas dance was well under way by the time Danny arrived at school. He shuffled along the corridor that led away from reception, the sound of blaring music belching from the school assembly hall ahead. A gaggle of little S1 girls in pretty pastel frocks came skipping towards him, giggling and laughing, silver and green and red tinsel entwined in their hair, not a care in the world. He veered away from them, took off his red cagoule and hung it on the coat hooks in the cloakroom. The S1's took a right turn and disappeared into the Girls' toilet. Danny was envious of their happy-go-lucky festive jollity and proceeded to trudge on towards the double doors of the hall, a sinister black mouth that he was certain was about to swallow him up and spit him out. Mr Ferry was standing by the portal of doom, arms folded, looking bored out of his wits.

'Afternoon, Danny,' he shouted over the raucous racket from within. 'You're a bit behind the curve this afternoon. All your friends are in there, bopping and boogeying away, having a whale of a time. You'd better get yourself in there.'

Danny tried to avoid eye contact, keeping his head down, but he sensed Ferry had momentarily glanced sideways at his radiator face.

'Afternoon, sir. Better get in there quick then, eh?' he muttered and slid by him just as Slade were vamping out the opening chords and Noddy Holder was asking the immortal question, 'Are you hanging up your stocking on the wall?'

Never in his life had Danny's senses been bombarded in such an all-consuming way as he stepped over the threshold between sanity and madness. The swirling, spiralling disco lights, the sonic boom of amplified pop, the stifling viscous heat, the pungent muskiness of teenage sweat, the tartness of cheap perfume and after-shave – overpowering, breath-taking, stupefying and wondrous. He didn't know whether to dive headlong into it or run all the way back to Faifley. When the crescendo built to Slade's chorus, 'So here it is Merry Christmas', he was buffeted and battered by a surging wave of frenzied pogoing, hundreds of faces screaming festive cheer to the rafters, arms held aloft in wild abandonment. He managed to zigzag his way to the side of the dance floor, weaving in and out of swirls of happiness, eddies of blissful exhilaration, raw youthful vitality in full swing and let loose on the world.

He was sweating. He was sweating profusely. The double curse of the polo neck affliction and the vest underneath was cooking him, roasting him like a scrawny turkey in an oven. The intense itching of the coarse wool on his upper chest reminded him of when he had chicken pox – he desperately wanted to scratch at himself but knew it would just make matters worse. Suddenly an arm grabbed him, a female arm. It was a second-year girl - he'd seen her before but didn't have clue what her name was – blond, cute, denim flares, white plimsoles, floral blouse with a collar you could go hang-gliding with. She was jumping up and down to the beat, screaming, 'Look to the future now, it's only just begun', holding Danny's arms and hauling him from side to side and every which way. Ominously, she also had a sprig of mistletoe in her hand.

The sweat increased.

Dancing with a girl the year below was a big no-no. Basically it was considered cheating, baby snatching and there was an unwritten rule that if you winched someone in S2, it wasn't a proper winch and you'd be branded for evermore as a deviant. Strangely, though, if you pulled someone in the year above, you'd be a hero.

More sweating.

Another repeat of the chorus.

The polo neck was now starting to sag under the weight of moisture being generated by O'Connell's gyrations. Just as Slade's rallentando of the climactic lines reached its cadence, he could take it no more. He grabbed the bottom edge of his polo neck and attempted to haul it over his head. Unfortunately for Danny, the narrow neckline smothered his face and he staggered about for a few seconds blind and disorientated, now a headless scrawny turkey in an oven. He continued to pull and drag at the confounded jumper, the coarse material scraping and scratching his coupon this way and that until finally, like some deformed butterfly emerging from a cocoon, he released himself from his straitjacket.

For a second, Danny was seeing stars and had to shake his head to compose himself. The S2 girl was standing in front of him, mistletoe loaded, ready to spring. Danny smiled at her and then a funny thing happened. She looked at him a little more closely. There in front of her stood a skinny beanpole with a sodden brown jumper in hand, his weedy chest encased in a white vest atop black corduroys whose trouser legs had a seam down the middle of them. What was more disconcerting was the boy's face, which now seemed to have melted, a dirty beige sludge smudged across his forehead and cheeks, beneath which was a countenance, lobster like, seemingly blistered and pox-ridden, and eyes that had a passing resemblance to a racoon.

She dropped the mistletoe, turned and ran into the relative safety of the crowd just as 'It'll be Lonely This Christmas' started spinning on the turntable.

'Holy crap. Whit happened to yir ugly mug, Danny. It's even uglier than before. I never thought that wid be possible.'

Charlie had appeared beside him, resplendent in his Bay City Rollers' gear. With his platforms on, he was nearly as tall as Danny and, with this height advantage he could see his friend in all his sartorial splendour.

'An' whit in the hell are you wearin'? Who comes tae a school dance wearing a vest? I mean just a vest. Your parents must be stoney broke after aw.'

'I was wearing this,' replied Danny and held up what seemed to be a sopping wet brown hessian sack.

'Christ, Danny. I see whit ye mean. The vest wins oot there, mate. That thing looks like somethin' a coo shat oot its erse.'

'Never mind me, Charlie. I'm a lost cause. How have you been daein? Have you scored yet? Any winchin'?'

'Aye, well, that's the thing, Danny. I've got a wee confession tae make. I hope ye don't take this the wrong way but I thought I'd have a wee crack at Catherine Mathieson.'

Danny glowered at him.

'All's fair in love and war an' aw that. And ye never really went oot wi' her, anyway, did ye?

'Aye, no thanks tae you.'

'Well, maybes aye, maybes naw.'

'So, go on then, make my day and tell me ye scored.'

'No' exactly. I went over tae her wi' the mistletoe – she's looking dead gorgeous today as well – all dolled up – and she saw me coming.'

'Did she make a run for it?'

'Naw, she walked up tae me aw sexy like and stared intae my eyes.'

'Aye she's good at the starin', for sure.'

'I lifted my sprig over her heid, puckered my lips and moved in for the kill.'

'Aw, shite, my worst nightmare.'

'Naw, it's no whit ye think… she slapped me right across the coupon. A right stinger it wis. Said she's rather die than kiss me. I wis the cause of the Tommy Lang incident and, of course The Stinky Knickers catastrophe. I don't think she saw the funny side o' it, Danny. Bit humourless if ye ask me. Anyways, we're better aff withoot her, eh?'

'O'Connell – what are you doing standing there in your vest? Have you no shame? Cover yourself immediately.'

Gleeson was standing behind them, his fingers twitching, itching to reach into his 'holster'. The figure in front of him offended his sense of decency and, if it hadn't been Christmas, he would have molocated O'Connell.

'Sorry, sir. Right away sir.'

Danny wriggled his way back into his wet and hairy cocoon, the sodden wool clinging to his back and chest.

'Aw, this is mingin', man. I've had enough o'this, Charlie boy. I'm heading for the exit.'

'Aye, fair enough big man. I can hardly walk in these platforms anyways. I feel as if I'm aboot tae coup over. How women can walk in high heels I'll never know. Let's head back tae mine and play 'Flying Hamster.''

The two boys weaved their way through the throng, Charlie tottering on his fashionable feet, Danny relieved that he would soon breathe fresh air again. They left the mayhem behind just as Mud's lead singer crooned into the heavens:

Merry Christmas, darling, wherever you are.

11

TROUBLES COME IN BATTALIONS

Danny was having a bad day. In the league table of bad days at school this was sitting right there at the top. As he sat with Charlie at the back of the Maths class, last period on the Wednesday afternoon, his shoulders were slumped and he looked at his hands, red raw and throbbing. The most galling thing was, none of it had been his fault, just one of those wrong place, wrong time situations. Added to this was the horrible prospect of Gleeson handing back their S3 Maths tests. Danny, having gone through the ordeal a couple of days beforehand, was in no rush to find out the result. Again, due to circumstances beyond his control, he knew this was not going to end well.

'Are ye aw right, big man?' enquired Charlie, uncharacteristically showing a sensitive empathy towards his pal.

'It's aw a bit shite, Charlie,' replied Danny. 'This place really sucks sometimes.'

Since their paths hadn't crossed that day because of subject choices and, with Danny's involvement in the school musical at break and lunchtime, Charlie was unaware of the little dramas that had unfolded during the course of Danny's day.

It had all started that morning with Peter Pettigrew, Peter Short-Arsed Pettigrew, the pint-sized pugilist who wanted to take on the world. Since half way through S2, when the rest of the boys in his year group had started to stretch and sprout, (some, like Danny, at an alarming rate) young Peter's resentment towards taller boys grew exponentially. For some inexplicable reason, every Wednesday morning, Pettigrew lay in wait by the school gates, a diminutive predator waiting for his prey. Whenever he saw suitable quarry, the taller the better, he would jump out and challenge them to a fight. The 'wee man' syndrome had always been recognised as a fact of life in the West of Scotland but Pettigrew took the wee 'boy' syndrome, paradoxically, to new heights.

'Hey, ya big fud,' he would say as an opening gambit, 'so ye think ye're a hard man, do yae?' Normally a 'barney' at the school had time-honoured procedural formalities to them. The two fighters would square up to each other, face to face like two boxers at a weigh-in, and press foreheads against each other. This would be followed by a bit of pushing and shoving, and then the aggressor would wrap his arm around the other guy's neck and the two would stagger about the playground 'like two spent swimmers that do cling together'. More often than not, that would be the sum of its parts and the whole dispute would fizzle out. Occasionally, though, there really was a proper to-do. The ROSLA boys didn't mess about. They would grab their foe's hair, drag the head down to waist height, then direct a swift boot to the face. These clashes were generally very quick, very intense and very violent. They were, without fail, accompanied by a chorus of 'Fight! Fight! Fight!' from the excitable onlookers and, most of the time, either ended with the loser with a bloody nose and black eyes or a male teacher grabbing both offenders and dragging them off to a classroom where further punishment awaited.

Pettigrew's modus operandi was somewhat different. On account of being vertically challenged, he did not have the reach to grab his victim's hair so, depending on the angle of attack he would go for a sneaky kick to the testicles or a sly jab to the face. In the early days of his campaign, he had the element of surprise and would sometimes hit the bull's eye. Nowadays, however, his 'victims' would see Pettigrew coming and one swift punch to the head or kick in the goolies sorted him out. He had been beaten up more often than the local boxing club's punch bag and had been on the receiving end of quite a few nasty beatings from some of the more hardened thugs of the school. His little peaked nose was crooked and he had a high-pitched nasal whine that seemed to suggest that puberty was proving somewhat elusive to him. Yet, he kept coming back for more. As the rest of the boys grew, so the greater the desperation to prove himself became.

And, by a process of elimination, he had reached Danny on his list of lofties to be slain. Therefore, this particular morning, like a wee scrawny weasel lying in wait, he was crouched behind the bins by the school gates as O'Connell came plodding by, troubled, lost in thought.

Danny became aware of someone exclaiming, 'So ye think ye're a hard man, do yae?' and turned just in time to see the stunted fiend launching himself into the air and throwing a right hook at him. He managed to pull his face away slightly but Pettigrew caught his left ear and, for a second, there was a ringing sensation in his head. The bantam, buoyed by hitting his first target in months, circled around, ready for more.

'For Gods' sake, Pettigrew, ya wee shite. Piss aff and leave me alone. I've no' got time for this and, quite frankly, I'm really no' in the mood,' snarled Danny, holding his left ear and glowering at the wannabee gladiator in front of him.

'Aye, O'Connell, I always thought ye were a piece o' chicken shit. Now I know.'

Pettigrew ran straight at Danny. From somewhere deep inside O'Connell, a fountain of resentment and anger welled up. He dropped his bag, clenched his fist, thrust his arm upwards and caught his attacker with the most perfectly timed uppercut to the chin. Pettigrew flew into the air, landed on his back, smacked his head off the tarmac and lay still.

'Right O'Connell. I saw that. My office. Right away. You know school rules about fighting.'

It was the depute headmaster, Mr McLaren, Big Andy as the kids affectionately called him.

'But sir, he started it...'

'Heard it all before, O'Connell. All I know is you've banjoed Pettigrew and he's out cold. That's six o' the best comin' your way.'

Danny had managed to chart a way through the stormy waters of secondary school without running aground on the shores of Big Andy's office. He wasn't called Big for nothing. He was built like the side of the proverbial and anyone who had been on the receiving end of Big Andy's tawse had come out of the experience with a heightened sense of their own mortality.

And so it was with O'Connell. When he left the Depute's office ten minutes later (Pettigrew, having miraculously recovered, had merrily scuttled off to Techie Drawing, scot free) the deep sense of grievance was almost as scorching as his red-hot hands. On top of everything else that was going on in his life, this was just adding insult to injury. By the time he arrived at his English lesson, half the period had gone. He knocked on the door and went in.

There are some days in the dynamics of a classroom when, quite frankly, the devil's afoot and Auld Nick holds court. Today was one of those days. Danny had forgotten that they had a student teacher, Miss Russell, on Wednesday mornings and as chance would have it, she had been handed a hospital pass by their normal teacher, Mrs O'Neill, an old wizened septuagenarian whom the school had brought out of retirement for the umpteenth time because of a lack of English specialists available. You could tell she was old, really old school by the chalk encrusted academic gown that she wrapped herself in. She had given Miss Russell the unenviable task of teaching Act 4, scene 1 of 'Macbeth', the witches cauldron scene. Unfortunately for Danny, someone had just delivered the lines, 'By the pricking of my thumbs, Something wicked this way comes,' just as he opened the door. The timing of this for the class was obviously exquisite but the close juxtaposition of words like 'pricking' and 'comes' for the boys had already done the damage. They were in paroxysms of laughter, the girls not far behind. The fact that Miss Russell was a very attractive brunette who invariably blushed whenever there was any hint of sexual innuendo just added to the whole delicious confection of the moment.

'Stop that laughing, S3. Stop it immediately. This is not funny.'

Miss Russell, now screeching like one of the midnight hags in the play, just added fuel to the flames by insisting that the situation was not amusing. The kids just laughed even louder.

'This is serious drama. This is Shakespeare. Stop this. Stop it right now.'

Danny, still standing just inside the door, decided to get out of the line of fire and started sidling towards his seat at the back.

'You boy. Where do you think you are going? I want you to go and fetch Mrs O'Neill from the staffroom and bring her up here.'

'But miss...'

'NOW!' she screamed. 'And don't contradict me.'

Danny wasn't aware that he had been given the chance to

contradict her but the poor lassie had completely lost the plot, there was abject fear in her eyes and he had no option but to acquiesce.

Ten minutes later, with Mrs O'Neill crawling laboriously along the corridor like an old turtle, he knocked on the door again and entered.

The noise level had diminished fractionally but the atmosphere of mischief and mayhem remained hanging in the air. The look of terror was still etched on her face.

'Where have you been, boy! Where's Mrs O'Neill?'

O'Neill, just at that point, shuffled into the room, now looking more like an octogenarian after her exertions in rushing from the staffroom.

The two teachers looked at each other, five decades of experience separating them, yet still bound by an unwritten rule that you protect each other from the cultural Vandals and Visigoths, the little Barbarians who refuse to be civilised, the swine that rejected their pearls of wisdom. They stepped out of the classroom for a minute or so, during which time, Danny thought it prudent to sit down.

'Right,' squawked O'Neill as she re-entered the room, Russell having been relieved of duty and sent back to the staffroom. 'This is entirely unacceptable. This is not how we treat student teachers, this is not how we behave as human beings. I have never been more appalled and ashamed in all my 50 years of teaching. All of you, every single one of you, will be given two of the belt.'

A hand at the back of the class shot up. 'But miss, I wisnae part o' this. I wis just the messenger.'

'Methinks you do protest too much O'Connell. Four of the belt for you. Up you come, you're first.'

She was so old, she hardly had the strength to lift the belt never mind deliver the downward stroke but, having already been softened up by Big Andy, Danny's hands continued to sting and his sense of injustice intensified. What was even worse, after having belted all the boys first, she stopped, her emaciated frame simply worn out by the effort of delivering 36 blows of the Lochgelly. The final few swipes had been so weak they were like being caressed with a feather and the boys had difficulty in keeping a straight face.

'Right, let that be a lesson to you,' she declared.

'But miss, ye huvnae belted the lassies,' bleated on or two of the indignant boys.

Just at that point the bell rang.

'I'll deal with them later. Class dismissed.'

With much mumping and grumping, the boys shuffled towards the door. As Danny left, he looked over his shoulder at the dried up and desiccated old bat slumping wearily into her chair, the old adage, 'This is going to hurt me more than it hurts you,' springing into his mind.

Danny's sense of injury assuaged itself somewhat as the morning wore on and, by the time he walked into the Geography class first period after lunch, he was feeling a little less mutinous, though still a troubled soul. The Geography teacher, Mr Grady, was ordinarily competent, if somewhat full of himself. He was in his early 40's and didn't wear suits or tailored jackets, preferring open neck shirts, tank tops, corduroys and hiking boots. He also prided himself in his handle-bar moustache that seemed to lend a permanent grin to his features. This slightly maverick image had been further developed with the rumour that was flying around the school that he had left his wife recently and was now shacking up with a former pupil, a girl that had left school the previous year, the really juicy gossip being that the affair had started when she was in sixth year. This was, as they say, the talk of the steamie, and, that afternoon, with many of the pupils who were in Danny's English set also in this Geography set, there was still a whiff of mischievousness in the air.

'Right, we're going to revise the unit on contour lines this afternoon. Going by the evidence of your tests last week, you've all forgotten what the hell contour lines are.'

He turned to the blackboard.

'Aye, but you huvnae,' blurted out a voice from the other side of the class from Danny.

The class tittered as one.

'OK, who said that?' enquired Grady immediately, his brows furrowing, his eyes scanning the classroom for a guilty face. All eyes looked down at their desks.

'I'm going to count to ten and if no one owns up, the lot of you are getting the belt. 10...9...'

Danny groaned.

'8...7...'

He couldn't believe this.

'6...5...'

Three times in one day.

'4...3...'

Surely not.

'2...1... Right, you've all asked for it.'

He went to the top drawer in his desk and rummaged around in it. Danny had never seen Grady use the belt before - he generally had good control over the masses - so was slightly curious as to how this was going to pan out. After much guddling about and peering at the back of the drawer he extricated something from its depths. He held it up for all to see.

'This is a pinkie belt and you are all going to find out why,' he avowed.

It was a slim sliver of brown leather, no more than four inches long. From the boys, there was much sniggering and salacious sneering. What on earth did the sixth-year lassie see in him if that was the size of his belt?

'Right, I'll do it by rows. The row nearest the door - you're up first.'

Once again, Danny found himself in the first wave of casualties, his sense of martyrdom increasing by the second. He stood in front of Grady and held out his right hand for the sixth time that day.

'Just the pinkie,' stated Grady matter-of-factly as he hovered the tiny leather strip a few inches above O'Connell's small finger.

Suddenly, he whacked the tip of the pinkie and gestured to Danny to raise his left hand. He repeated the process.

Danny almost laughed out loud. He felt nothing. No sting, no tingle, no pain. He thought that maybe he had now become desensitised to the whole belting game. Having been whacked three times in a day was a novel experience for him. Even Charlie hadn't managed that accolade. As he was walking back to his desk, he suddenly noticed that the pupils who had been belted a few minutes before him were now behaving in a most peculiar manner. They were all blowing on their pinkie finger tips and waving their hands back and forth. One or two of the girls were starting to cry. He sat down – and then it started. The tips of his little fingers started to throb, a pain so intense it did indeed nearly bring a tear to his eye. With every heartbeat the ache grew worse, the agony localised, all the blood in his body seemingly rushing to the ends of his pinkies. It was excruciating. Now he understood who Grady was – a humourless, cold-blooded sadist.

And so, as he sat beside Charlie that afternoon in Maths, he asked his friend, 'If you dropped out of the frying pan into the fire, where's the worst place you could go after that?'

'Dunnow, Danny. You're being shat on frae a great height, that's for sure.'

'O'Connell!' bellowed Gleeson. 'What is this dog's dinner of a paper you've handed in? Half way through marking it and you've only managed 10 per cent.'

Now, if there was one thing Danny prided himself in, it was

doing well in exams, even Maths. He had never failed an exam in his life. Everyone in the class knew this and, as a consequence of this, everyone in the class turned and stared at him, some confused, many grinning, *schadenfreude* always in plentiful supply in the top sets.

'And there's another question wrong. Nul points on that page.'

Gleeson continued to give a sneering, snidey commentary on O'Connell's running score.

'Oh, hang on a minute. There's one right. What a surprise... Ah, but we're back to form. The next one's complete mathematical twaddle.'

By the end of marking the paper, Danny could only stare into the middle distance, battening down the hatches for the storm that was coming.

'Well, O'Connell, you really have surpassed yourself. So, S3. O'Connell's final score?'

Gleeson rattled his fingers on his desk in a mock drum roll, '20 percent.'

Incredulous murmuring and muttering rippled round the class.

'Top set Maths, O'Connell? Top set Maths? In your dreams.'

Just then, the bell rang and the rest of the pupils shuffled to their feet, packing their things away, glancing across at Danny who had a lump the size of a golf ball in his throat. He slowly packed his jotter, pens and pencils into his bag, shell-shocked, waiting for the class to thin out, unable to face questions and queries and taunts.

'Danny,' said Charlie quietly to him, 'Could you wait for me outside? I just want tae ask Gleeson aboot my paper. I don't know if he's marked it.'

'Aye, OK, Charlie. Nae bother.'

Danny stepped out of the classroom and stood on the other side of the door. He didn't want to walk down the corridor and run the gauntlet of his peers. The door remained ajar.

He heard Charlie's voice from inside.

'Mr Gleeson. Can I have a word, sir?'

'What is it Harkness. School day's over. Time to go.'

'I dinnae know if you realise but there's a reason Danny's cocked up his Maths paper.'

'Aye, it's because he mucks about with you at the back there.'

'Naw, naw. I know it's not his strongest subject but he always works hard tae catch up.'

'Obviously not hard enough. He'll be lucky to be in the third set after this.'

'Listen, Mr Gleeson. He phoned me the ither night there, the night before the Maths exam. He told me not tae tell anyone but I think you should know. His dad had a stroke and is in intensive care. He was given the last rites an' everythin' and he's just hangin' oan. Mr Gleeson, Danny's heid's mince at the moment. I don't think that wis fair tae embarrass him like that in front o' everyone else.'

'Are you telling me how to do my job, Harkness?'

'I'm just tellin' ye tae go easy on him, that's aw. His dad nearly died, for Gods'sake.'

'How dare you, Harkness. I'm beginning to think you've taken leave of your senses. No upstart third year is going to tell me how to run my class. Now get the hell out of here before I lose it with you.'

Charlie turned to go but then swung back to face Gleeson.

'Ye know, my mum went tae school wi' you and she said ye were a wee nyaff back then.'

'Right, Harkness. Put your hand out. No one speaks to me like that.'

'And do you know whit else she said? "Once a wee nyaff, always a wee nyaff."'

Charlie turned to go, as Gleeson stepped towards him.

'Come back here right now, Harkness. Right now.'

'Fuck off, sir. Just fuck off.'

Charlie stepped into the corridor and came face to face with Danny.

'Let's get out o' here, Danny.'

The two boys marched down the corridor side by side with Gleeson's shrill voice echoing off the bare walls.

'You haven't heard the end of this, Harkness.'

'Jesus, Charlie. Whit have ye done?'

'Ach well, Danny. He had it comin' tae him. Anyways, after the day you've had, I thought you could do wi' a laugh.'

12

JOSEPH

May I return to the beginning?
The light is dimming and the dream is too.
The world and I, we are still dreaming,
Still hesitating,
Any dream will do.

'Yeah, that's lovely, Michael. Absolutely spot on. You really nailed it there. OK, that's great. Just wanted to put the finishing touches to that bit and we're ready for the big one tomorrow night. Well done everyone and we'll see you all at 6.00 tomorrow evening.'

Mr Ferry clapped his hands together and smiled broadly. Months of practice, preparation, cajoling, sleepless nights and tetchy rehearsals had brought this ship within sight of land. Michael Devlin, a fresh-faced little cherub with an angelic voice, was the principal in 'Joseph and the Amazing Technicolor Dreamcoat', and had just crooned his way through the final verse of the final song, ironing out a few little bits of intonation and gesture. Ferry was always thorough, detail driven, leaving nothing to chance. He turned to look at Danny, sitting by the piano.

'Well done, Danny. The band was spot on there. Excited?'

'Aye Mr Ferry. I cannae wait for tomorrow night. The whole school's pure buzzing aboot it. It's a sell-oot, ye know.'

'Yes, that's great. Don't want to tempt fate but it deserves to be. Hope you got your allocation of tickets.'

'Aye, thanks. My dad's still no well enough tae get oot and aboot but my mum, my brother and sister'll be there.'

'Excellent. Well, here's hoping it'll pass the O'Connell's high artistic standards, eh, Danny?'

'Aye, nae bother, Mr Ferry, don't you worry aboot that.'

Danny grinned and packed up his music. He was on the acoustic piano, with Ferry on electric keyboards. The rest of the band was made up of members of staff, mainly PE teachers oddly enough, who were pretty handy on their chosen instruments. The cast and chorus had been gobsmacked when Mr Fahey, the young football coach, had sat down behind the drum kit the first day of full band rehearsals, his manual dexterity with the drumsticks dazzling them. Instantly he had a gaggle of groupie S3 girls following him everywhere about the school, staring at him, doe-eyed and star struck. Mr Collins, the athletics coach, and Mr Armstrong, head of PE, were lead and bass guitar respectively and they had their own fans, generally boys who were more interested in the type of guitars they played and their taste in music.

Never in the history of Danny's school had such an event taken place. Sure, there had been concerts and musical evenings, where kids stood rooted to the spot in starchy shirts and school ties, singing 'Step We Gaily On We Go' and 'Speed Bonnie Boat' and other worthy songs that grannies approved of and audience's attended out of duty. The choir was nearly always made up of girls, the lads regarding warbling out old Scottish folk songs as effeminate and sissified. But this was different.

This was a modern musical with catchy songs and funny lyrics, larger than life characters and the chance to sing and dance and mix with girls in costume - the boys signed up immediately.

The idea that a comprehensive school could actually mount a production of this magnitude was somewhat radical in this part of the world. Clydebank was not exactly world famous for its thespian interests, Christmas pantomimes being the limit of most Bankies' theatrical horizons. Indeed, the gainsayers and doom-mongers prophesied that it would be an unmitigated disaster, a comprehensive school with poor academic results in the heart of the industrial belt of Scotland not exactly perceived as a hotbed of artistic talent. Some thought it would be like trying to teach chimpanzees quadratic equations. Indeed, that is how Gleeson expressed it in the staffroom one day, telling Ferry that he would end up in a straitjacket with a one-way ticket to the funny farm if he persisted in his quixotic enterprise. There were two staffrooms, one male, one female, the former a yellow-tinged dingy, smoky, dive with threadbare carpets and the lingering aroma of stale man-sweat. Gleeson had his own chair by the window, an old leather armchair that no one else was allowed to occupy. He sat there as if holding court, his nicotine-stained fingers clasping a Benson and Hedges, drawing deeply on the cigarette, a sneer in the corner of his mouth.

'You're off your head, Ferry,' he declared at breaktime the morning that auditions had been announced. 'They're all wee shites, as you know. Talentless wee shites at that. In fact, lazy talentless wee shites. If you want to drive yourself into an early grave, this is one sure way of doing it.'

Ferry smiled. 'Thanks for the advice, John. I'll bear it in mind.'

But Ferry knew he was not tilting at windmills. He had taken over as Head of Music that academic session and, being young and idealistic, had faith in the transformative power of his subject. He also believed that in a school of 1200, there would be talent to be unearthed. Sure, there was currently only one pupil that was taking certificate Music in S3 – Danny O'Connell – but he believed implicitly that if you looked hard enough and provided opportunity, the kids would respond. You just had to give them something they could embrace. Hence 'Joseph and the Amazing Technicolor Dreamcoat', the perfect musical starter-kit for laying the foundations of a musical metamorphosis in a school. He also had the added advantage of being an exceptional pianist himself. The kids were in awe of his talent – whether it was classical or rock, he could turn his hand to it and, where there is musical flair, kids will follow.

And so, after months of hard work and perseverance, he had just finished the dress rehearsal and knew that this would all be worth it. The one and only performance would be the following Saturday night, a week before the end of the summer term. As Ferry packed his stuff into his car, Gleeson was walking towards his Ford Cortina. Ferry turned and quietly said, 'You should try teaching that chimpanzee quadratic equations some time, John. It might be quite liberating for you.'

'Piss off, Ferry. Don't count your chickens. The little bleeders'll let you down. It's in their DNA.'

'Well, I hope you'll be there to see my downfall, John. I'm sure it will appeal to your sense of balance and proportion.'

'Oh, I'll be there all right. Don't you worry about that. Somebody has to keep order.'

Danny stood in the central aisle of the assembly hall the following night at 6.30, row upon row of steel framed wooden chairs to his left and right, the house lights dimmed, one follow spot shining brightly on the middle of the stage curtains. He had barely slept the night before, playing over and over in his mind the chronological order of the songs, watching his hands as if they were detached from his body running over the black and white keys, replaying over and over the tricky fingering in some of the more technical instrumental sections. In the wee small hours as he drifted off into that twilight zone half way between sleep and consciousness he watched in horror as some of the characters in the musical came on stage and sang other characters' songs, muddling up lines, missing cues, the whole production descending into farce and anarchy. He knew sub-consciously that this was all wrong but seemed powerless to stop it.

But now, standing there in real time and space, it all made sense. Mr Ferry was plugging in the keyboard, Mr Armstrong and Mr Collins were adjusting the volume on their amps and Mr Fahey had just managed to extricate himself from a posse of S3 girls hanging about at the hall entrance, all dressed to kill, all hoping that the drummer boy would speak to them, even just look at them. Slightly flustered, Fahey crossed the hall floor, sat on his stool and took out his drums.

Danny had taken part in concerts before but this was a whole new experience. And he knew, right there, right then, that something had changed in his life, a Pauline conversion – he was born to do this. You could take your Latin and your French and your History and your Geography and shove them in the rubbish bin of vocations. This is what called to him; this is what would define him.

Like the kids who had stepped through the wardrobe into Narnia, he had, earlier, slid behind the curtain and gone backstage into another world where Egyptians, Israelites, Pharaohs, bakers, butlers, American cheerleaders, girls in grass skirts, Go-Go Dancers and camels were all wandering about. He had to do a double-take when a Hairy Ishmaelite smiled at him and said, 'Evening Danny!' It was Clooney the Looney's eyes looking out from behind the most hirsute beard he had ever seen. 'Evening, sir,' replied Danny. 'That look suits you, sir.' Clooney guffawed, Danny astounded by the blurring of traditional roles, the fact that this man who had given him six of the belt not so long ago could let slide a pupil's comment on how he looked and actually get away with it.

But the whole thing was like that. Female members of staff were laughing and joking with kids as they applied stage make-up, Danny ruefully remembering the last time make-up played a part in his life, in this exact venue just six months before. Miss Russell, the student teacher, was helping out with costumes, making last minute adjustments and tweaking hems and shoulder straps, the trauma of the cauldron scene a distant memory. The sound and lighting team, boys and techie teachers, were sitting side by side doing last minute checks. At the back of the hall, high up on a rickety looking scaffolding tower, there was Big Andy and wee McFud, little and large, holding on to the huge follow spot. Everywhere Danny looked he saw teamwork between young and old delivered with smiles, chortles, merriment and laughs. Underpinning it all was a nervous excitement, a frisson of energy, a sweet anticipation – why couldn't school always be like this, wondered Danny: no bullying, no belting, no them and us.

'OK, Danny, quick sound check,' Ferry called to him and pulled him out of his reverie. As they plonked and twanged and rolled, making last minute adjustments, Danny was aware that the hall was beginning to fill, the sound of chatter and babble rippling round the walls. He was side-on to the audience and, being on floor level, had not appreciated how close they would actually be to him. His palms started to become moist.

'Aw right, ya big Dunkie's whalloper?' Charlie appeared suddenly at his side.

'Aw right, Charlie boy? This is the dog's whatsits, innit.'

'Aye, looking forward tae it, big man. Get tae see whit the hell you've been daen the last wee while.'

Charlie had not signed up for the musical – it would have interrupted his golfing schedule - but he was keen to find out what all the buzz was in the school. Just at that point, Danny caught sight of a dark and morose figure standing at the back of the hall. Gleeson was leaning against the scaffolding tower glowering malevolently at the scene in front of him.

'Aw, Christ, Charlie. There's Gleeson back there. Just watch yirsel'.'

'Ach, don't you worry aboot him. He's not goin' tae make waves. I reckon he never told anyone aboot whit I said tae him – he'd be cacking himself the thought that others knew he wis bang oot o'order and that he lost control. He's too up himsel' tae lose face. Anyways. I'm untouchable, noo.'

'How come?'

'I just won the Scottish Schoolboys this afternoon. I'm top golfer for my age in the country, Danny boy.'

'Aw, bloody hell, Charlie. That's pure dead brilliant, that is. Well done ya jammy wee shite.'

'Raw talent, Danny. Raw talent. Anyways, the school arnae gonnae touch me. Too much good publicity, eh? Right, you'd better get oan wi' it. Break a finger, Danny.'

'It's break a leg, Charlie, ya muppet.'

'Oan yersel, big man.'

The lights dimmed; the audience settled; the band struck up. The next hour and a quarter was the fastest 75 minutes Danny had ever experienced. Mr Ferry had told him that there was real time and stage time, that he should enjoy the moment because it would fly by in the blink of an eye and how right he was. It did not go without a hitch – the little moments of unforeseen snags that make live theatre experience all the more fulfilling and vibrant nonetheless. When Jacob's beard started to peel away from the left side of the face just as he was being told of Joseph's demise, a few of the brothers corpsed, much to the delight of the audience; when one of the camels lost its bearings trying to exit the stage and kept colliding with the proscenium arch, the crowd applauded with gusto; when Mr Brundell, dressed as Onion Johnny, rode his bicycle up the central aisle too quickly, lost his balance and crashed into the headmaster sitting in the front row the roof nearly caved in; when a blow up palm tree decided to deflate as the boys pleaded, 'Benjamin is straighter than the tall palm tree' even Danny had difficulty in concentrating on his music such was the power of his giggling fit.

But aside from these moments of hilarity, the audience was spell-bound, mothers and fathers and grannies and grandpas, aunties and uncles and brothers and sisters, all entranced by an ancient bible story set to rockn'roll music. They even forgot for a while that they were watching their own offspring or siblings such is the power of theatre to move and mesmerise. If Ferry had been able to distil the pure unadulterated joy of escapism in the hall that night, he would have found the elixir of life.

By the time the encores were called for, Danny just wanted to perform the whole show all over again. He beamed at Mr Ferry who seemed to be hovering slightly above the floor, buoyed up by the cheering and the clapping and the whistling and the shouts of 'Bravo.' A whole school brought together as one, humanity at is best. And when Pharaoh walked on stage in his Elvis outfit to reprise his showstopper, the sheet pane glass windows of the hall rattled and rocked and nearly exploded outwards. A member of the audience stood up. Danny thought he saw Gleeson making a move to push him back into his chair, but then another and another and another got to their feet as Pharaoh launched into 'Hey, hey, hey Joseph'. The whole hall was standing, a mother a couple of rows from the front was in tears, mascara dripping down her face, pointing at the gyrating Elvis look-a-like and was screaming at the top of her voice, 'That's my boy. That's my boy.' Big Andy and wee McFadden were bouncing up and down on a wooden plank on top of scaffolding that looked as if it was about to topple over, the follow spot not following anything in particular. By the final cadence the rafters shook and the floor quaked.

It was all over. The audience did not want leave. The kids on stage did not want to exit stage left and stage right. There was an awkward stand-off until the headmaster stood up and signalled for all to go.

Down the side aisle nearest to him, Danny suddenly saw his brother and sister, seemingly swimming against the tide, trying to clear a way for his mum who suddenly appeared out of the throng pushing Danny's dad in a wheel chair. He had made it, after all.

'Well done, Daniel, that was outstanding,' his mum declared, smiling broadly.

Not known for being particularly tactile, Danny was taken aback when mother, sister and brother all gave him a big hug. His dad, a moist tear in his eye, simply whispered, 'Well done, son.'

Danny's mum turned to Mr Ferry.

'Mr Ferry, I'd just like to thank you for everything you've done for my son. You have been an inspiration to him and the school. Thank you so much.'

'Don't mention it, Mrs O'Connell. You've got a great kid there. You should be proud.'

Danny's mum smiled and nodded, then turned back to her son.

'Well, I believe there is some sort of after-show party, so I assume we'll see you later.'

'Are you giving me permission to go, mum?'

'Just this once, Daniel. Just this once.'

As the audience thinned out and he packed away his libretto, out of the corner of his eye, he saw Gleeson slink out of the side exit, head down, shoulders hunched. It dawned on Danny that he was watching a man who would never be able to comprehend what had just happened, that what was creeping away into the night was the past, a damaged, damaging generation of teachers whose days were numbered. Standing beside him, having a beer with the other band members, was the future, a breath of fresh air, enlightened and full of humanity.

He suddenly became aware of a figure beside him. It was a radiant angel in white vestments and the angel was carrying a cardboard harp spray-painted gold. This vision of loveliness was Catherine Mathieson and she was smiling at him.

'Hi Danny. I thought you were brilliant tonight on the piano. Yer so talented.'

Danny blushed and didn't quite know where to look.

'I thought you were super as well. The way ye glided across the stage. Pure class.'

'Och, it was only a walk on part. I cannae sing, I cannae act and I cannae play an instrument.'

'Aye but ye look good wi' a cardboard harp.'

She laughed. 'Are ye going tae the party? If so, do ye want tae go with me?'

'Aye for sure, Catherine.'

'Call me Cathy. All my friends do.'

Danny beamed from ear to ear.

'Hey O'Connell, ya big muppet. Are ye gonnae be there all night?

Charlie was walking towards him with an even bigger smile on his face. He had his arm around the waist of Anne-Marie Reardon.

'Anne-Marie's just asked me tae the party. Whit dae ye make o' that?'

'I guess it's yer lucky day Charlie – and mine.'

Charlie nodded at Catherine Mathieson, not sure what to say, considering the last contact he had with her was the palm of her hand on his face.

'Are we awright, Catherine?'

'Aye, no problems, Charlie. It's all forgotten now, isn't Danny.'

'Don't know whit yer bletherin' aboot, guys. Let's go and have fun.'

As they all turned to head down the central aisle, Danny noticed a small figure standing on the stage looking out at where the audience had been. It was the wee S2 boy who had played Joseph and he was crying his eyes out.

'Hey, kid. Are ye awright?' asked Danny looking up at him from floor level.

'Aye Danny, I'm fine. I just don't want the happiness tae end, that's aw. I just don't want it tae end.'

'Aye, right enough. I know whit ye mean.'

Danny turned and slipped his arm around Catherine's waist. After all, if Charlie could do it, so could he. As he walked down the aisle with her, Charlie behind him with his girl, he began to sing and, as he did so, they all joined in:

I wore my coat, with golden lining
Bright colours shining, wonderful and new,
And in the east, the dawn was breaking,
And the world was waking
Any dream will do.

ACKNOWLEDGEMENTS

Firstly, I'd like to thank my brilliant wife, Mary, for all the hard work, patience, resilience and sheer dogged determination in bringing this book to fruition. I might have done the creative bit but that is the just the tip of the iceberg. Thank you so much for your love and dedication.

Secondly, a big thanks to Charlie Mcdonald for all the years of fun we've shared together and being the source of many of these stories. Our journey and friendship continue. A special mention to Carol, his wife, for providing feedback in Vilamoura last year. Your infectious laughter made me believe in the project.

Thirdly, my children, Ciaran and Erin, who had to listen to these stories from their old man over the years so many times before I actually committed them to paper.

Next, my brother, Quinton, and his wife, Marian, for your supportive comments when I ran these stories past you during lockdown. Our weekly videocalls were always the highlight of the week.

A big thanks to my sister, Clare, and my cousin, Hector Cairns, whose advice and feedback helped me improve my writing style.

I'd also like to thank Victoria Twead and Ant Press for all your help, advice and support. It has been fascinating seeing how the wheels of publishing turn and your professionalism has been outstanding.

Finally, a tip of the hat to all the teachers and pupils in the 1970s at St Columba's High School, Clydebank, without whom, none of this would have existed.

ABOUT THE AUTHOR

Patrick George O'Kane, born and raised in the West Coast of Scotland. He emerged from the Scottish education system with an Honours Degree (in English Language and Literature) from Glasgow University. He became Head of English at Morrison's Academy, retiring recently to travel the world and scribble profundities about the human condition.

When at home, in his beloved town of Crieff, he can be spotted either jogging across the Perthshire hillsides or manically chasing a wee white ball around the local golf course.

Patrick is currently working on a psychological thriller, *A Semblance of Trust*, and planning a follow-up to *Joining the Dots*.

CONTACTS AND LINKS

Facebook: facebook.com/patrickgeorgeokane

Instagram: @pgokaneauthor

Printed in Great Britain
by Amazon

30974555R00086